"I'd be happy to keep you company tonight."

Marilou's skin burned at Cal's deliberately provocative invitation. "Thanks, but you probably snore."

"You'll never know till you spend the night with me."

"I could always bug your room instead."

He chuckled at the quick retort. "You know, most women would have been scared off," he said.

"I've told you before, you don't scare me," she responded lightly, ignoring the rapid thudding of her heart. She had detected a very faint and very reluctant note of admiration in his voice. "You're all bluff."

There was a quick flash of amusement in his eyes before he began a slow, deliberate inspection. Her pulse hammered and heat rose through her before she finally shifted her gaze away. No man's look had ever been so blatantly seductive.

"I wouldn't call my bluff if I were you," he warned, still not taking his eyes off her. "You might get more than you bargained for...."

D0596346

Dear Reader,

Welcome to Silhouette **Special Edition** . . . welcome to romance. Each month Silhouette **Special Edition** publishes six novels with you in mind—stories of love and life, tales that you can identify with— romance with that little ''something special'' added in.

And this month is no exception to the rule. May 1991 brings *No Quarter Given* by Lindsay McKenna—the first in the thrilling WOMEN OF GLORY series. Don't miss more of this compelling collection coming in June and July. Stories by wonderful writers Curtiss Ann Matlock, Tracy Sinclair, Sherryl Woods, Diana Stuart and Lorraine Carroll (with her first **Special Edition!**) round out this merry month.

In each Silhouette **Special Edition**, we're dedicated to bringing you the romances that you dream about— the type of stories that delight as well as bring a tear to the eye. And that's what Silhouette **Special Edition** is all about—special books by special authors for special readers!

I hope you enjoy this book and all of the stories to come.

Sincerely,

Tara Gavin
Senior Editor

SHERRYL WOODS
My Dearest Cal

Silhouette Special Edition

Published by Silhouette Books New York

America's Publisher of Contemporary Romance

For Craig, Dianne, Michael and Kelly
for all the holiday family dinners and
for the insight into postal regulations.
For Ken, Eddie, Matda, Fred and all the rest,
who brighten the endless time
an author seems to spend at the mailbox.
And especially for Nona, with thanks
for sharing your love of horses with me and
in memory of your beloved and gallant Bolshoi.

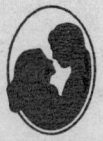

SILHOUETTE BOOKS
300 East 42nd St., New York, N.Y. 10017

MY DEAREST CAL

ISBN: 0-373-09669-0

First Silhouette Books printing May 1991

Printed in the U.S.A.

Books by Sherryl Woods

Silhouette Desire

Not at Eight, Darling #309
Yesterday's Love #329
Come Fly with Me #345
A Gift of Love #375
Can't Say No #431
Heartland #472
Next Time...Forever #601
Fever Pitch #620

Silhouette Special Edition

Safe Harbor #425
Never Let Go #446
Edge of Forever #484
In Too Deep #522
Miss Liz's Passion #573
Tea and Destiny #595
My Dearest Cal #669

Silhouette Books

Silhouette Summer Sizzlers 1990
"A Bridge to Dreams"

SHERRYL WOODS

lives by the ocean, which, she says, provides daily inspiration for the romance in her soul. She further explains that her years as a television critic taught her about steamy plots and humor; her years as a crummy weekend tennis player taught her to stick with what she enjoyed most—writing. "What better way is there," Sherryl asks, "to combine all that experience than by creating romantic stories?"

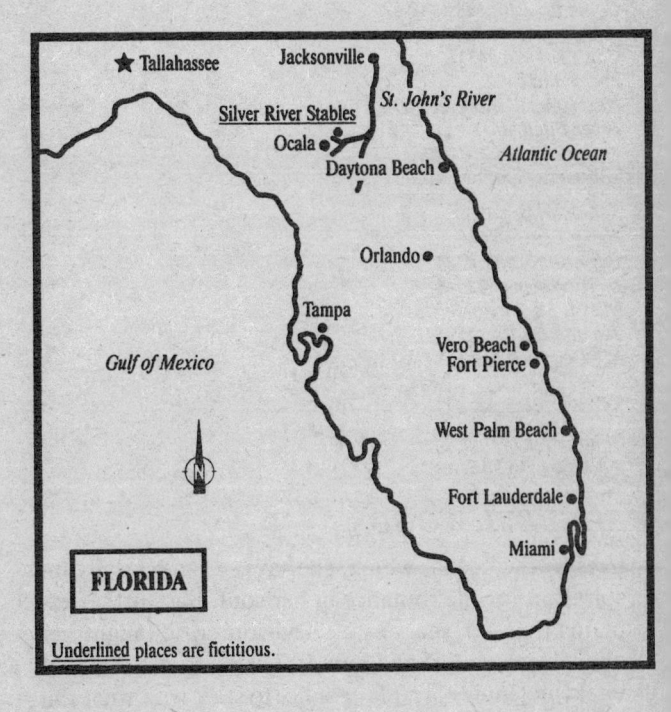

★ Tallahassee

Jacksonville

<u>Silver River Stables</u>

St. John's River

Ocala

Daytona Beach

Atlantic Ocean

Orlando

Tampa

Gulf of Mexico

Vero Beach
Fort Pierce

West Palm Beach

N

Fort Lauderdale

Miami

FLORIDA

<u>Underlined</u> places are fictitious.

Chapter One

April showers, Marilou thought with a disgusted sniff. She splashed through an ankle-deep puddle on her way to work. At this rate the poor May flowers would drown. She sneezed and shivered as a chilly Thursday morning wind scooped up the hem of her raincoat and lifted it just high enough to allow the rain to drench her new red skirt. Drown, hell. They'd probably freeze first.

It must be warm and sunny someplace right now, she thought longingly as she trudged across the parking lot toward her office. Wherever it was, she would give anything to be there. Tahiti. Hawaii. Even the Sahara. It didn't much matter as long as it was dry. And hot. The winter in Atlanta had been the pits. It was now one week into the dreariest, wettest April on record. Judging from the endless gray sky, spring obviously wasn't going to be much of an improvement.

A few minutes later, still sneezing and blowing her nose, Marilou settled into her cubbyhole in the U.S. Postal Service's Dead Letter Office and grimly faced the stacks of unopened mail that had gone astray in the Southeast. Whole shelves around her held everything from lost keys to movie reels, all silent testimony to the carelessness of people in a hurry. A red bikini top dangled from a hook—the bottom had vanished. One of her co-workers had hung the provocative garment where he could see it as he worked. She had a hunch Matt thoroughly enjoyed imagining the woman who'd been wearing it and the no doubt fascinating story behind its loss and subsequent discovery in some corner mailbox.

Normally Marilou started the day with enthusiasm, liking the challenge of reuniting letters and parcels with the intended recipients. She'd only been at it a little more than a year and a half, but so far she'd never found it tedious. It was a little like she imagined detective work would be. Getting treasured photos or a favorite teddy bear back to its rightful owner required the same kind of ingenuity and persistence it took to track missing persons or lost heirs. It was also emotionally rewarding, even if the person never knew about her involvement. Once in a while, like the time she'd gotten several thousand dollars worth of stock certificates back where they belonged, she'd received letters of praise and heartfelt thanks. This wasn't the adventurous life she'd once envisioned for herself, but it was good.

Usually, she amended with a sigh.

Today, however, with her shoes soaked again and her feet icy cold, she was in no mood to be sympathetic to the people who'd forgotten to put return addresses on their envelopes. She was tired of trying to decipher ink that had run after getting drenched by rain. She was out of patience with people who stuck their bills in backward so that the company address wasn't visible. And she'd had it up to her stuffed nose with idiots who figured they'd just send off their tax forms with no postage. As a protest against the IRS, it was useless. The forms went back to the sender, once she'd wasted half a day tracking them down. All in all, she felt like throwing the whole mess from her desk straight into the shredder, but she was too darned conscientious.

She shivered, then took one last sip of hot coffee before reaching for the one envelope that showed any promise. Addressed by a seemingly shaky hand to a Mr. Cal Rivers, it had been sent to an address in Florida that apparently didn't exist. "No such address" had been stamped emphatically across the front and again on the back.

Palm Tree Lane. Oh, how she liked the sound of that. Where there were palm trees, there was probably sunshine. Maybe even temperatures above the freeze-your-butt variety. Honest-to-gosh spring temperatures. She paused a minute to savor the very idea of lying on some sun-kissed stretch of sand, baking until she could actually breathe again.

When she finally got around to opening the letter, she was already feeling better just for having taken that brief mental vacation. But as she quickly scanned the thick vellum pages, filled with their crimped scrawl of words, her spirits sank once more. There was no return address anywhere. And although she wasn't supposed to read the contents, one or two phrases caught her eye—"Never forget that I love you...so sorry we've never had a chance to get to know each other...I'm dying now..."

Oh, my God. *Dying!* Knowing it was against every rule, Marilou went back to the beginning. "My dearest Cal..."

Now that she knew the ending, every word was so poignant, it made her want to weep. It seemed to be a farewell letter from a grandmother to a grandson she'd never met. Filled with longing and regrets, it broke Marilou's heart. The terrible, unexpected loss of her own parents was still new and raw, even after nearly eighteen months. There had been so many things left unsaid between them, so many arguments that would never be resolved. She ached at the thought that some little boy might have family he didn't even know about. There had to be a way to see that this letter reached him, that the family was reunited before it was too late.

Filled with determination, she hunted through the pile of phone books from every state in the region until she found the one she wanted. Please, just this once, let it be easy, she thought as she flipped through the pages to the Rs. Let this kid be named after his father. Or at the very least, let there not be twenty-five listings for Rivers. Rivas. Rivero—at least fifty of them. Then she found it. Rivers, Cal. Two-twenty-nine Palm Lane. Not Palm *Tree* Lane. What was the big deal? she thought indignantly. Some fool mailman couldn't figure out what the dear old woman meant?

Marilou reached for the phone, punched in the area code and number, only to hear the dreaded sound that always preceded some recorded message. With a sinking sensation, she anticipated this one.

"...Has been disconnected." Of course. No new number. Just disconnected.

She flipped back through the directory for the phone number of the local post office, called and asked if there was any record of a Cal Rivers leaving a forwarding address.

"It's not in the computer," the disinterested clerk told her eventually.

"Maybe it just expired. There should be a record..."

"I'm telling you it's not in here. For all I know it was never in here."

"Couldn't you..."

"Lady, I don't have all day to hunt for things that don't exist."

"What about the carrier for that route? Maybe he'd remember."

"That's probably Priscilla."

"Could I speak to her?"

"She's off today," the clerk said in a tone that ended any further discussion.

"Thanks for your help," Marilou said sarcastically into the already-dead connection. Apparently sunshine wasn't a guaranteed panacea for the ill tempers of the world.

She put the letter aside and went through the remaining stack of mail. One after another she was able to identify either sender or recipient and get the mail back on track. Those that were hopeless, actually the greatest percentage, went into the shredder. But even as she efficiently handled her usual hundreds of letters, that one brief note from Cal Rivers' grandmother began to haunt her.

According to regulations she was supposed to dispose of the letter since her search for sender and recipient had been unsuccessful. Only when there was something of value was the post office required to hold it for a year. In her mind, though, there really was something of value—a link to family, a cry for forgiveness. It might not have a dollar value, but to her way of thinking there was nothing more important. She couldn't bring herself to throw the letter away.

She understood that her obsession had everything to do with those last few days with her parents, days clouded with petty arguments and misunderstandings. When they'd left on their vacation, tensions had been running high. Marilou was their much-loved and overly protected only daughter. They hadn't wanted her to take off for Europe for a year without a job, without friends. Always skeptical that her photography was a sensible career choice, they'd been certain that she'd starve while trying to sell the pictures she shot on her travels. After a lifetime of secure government service, the concept of free-lancing was beyond them. Nothing she'd said had been able to persuade them that the time was right for a few risks, for one glorious post-college adventure before settling down.

With the last bitter argument still fresh in her mind, Marilou had been devastated by the news that they'd been involved in a head-on collision with a stolen car filled with teenagers on a joyride. Her father had been killed outright. Her mother had lingered on for several horrifying weeks, never regaining consciousness.

In the emotional aftermath of the tragedy and in an attempt to cheat fate, she had resigned herself to staying as safe as her parents had wanted. The bribe hadn't worked, her mother had died anyway. When the family savings had been depleted by the exorbitant medical bills, and when the last of her energy was drained, the civil service job had been waiting for her, thanks to her father's career with the post office and his compassionate supervisor. She told herself she should be grateful to have it.

With an odd sort of lethargy, Marilou had settled down to a routine, but the longing for adventure, for a chance to use her photographic skills for more than holiday snapshots had never quite gone away. Every foreign stamp that crossed her desk stirred all of the old dreams of travel. Every letter gone astray reminded her of the mysteries that awaited. The plea for forgiveness from Cal Rivers' grandmother tapped into every one of her secret longings and regrets.

That night when a passing bus hit a giant puddle and soaked her from head to toe, she made up her mind. She had weeks of vacation coming. She had a healthy savings account again. She had a cold. And, most of all, she had those unfulfilled dreams.

So, she decided impulsively, she was going to Florida in search of Mr. Cal Rivers and his little boy. That child probably needed a grandmother as desperately as that poor dying lady needed to be in touch with him. Marilou might not be able to get her own family back, but maybe she could give him his. If she got a taste of adventure along the way, so much the better.

"Crazy, obstinate, mule-headed son of a bitch! Get in here. What kind of genes do you have anyway? Any other fool would be dancing and prancing to get a chance to be with that gorgeous lady in there. That little gal's folks paid a pretty penny for you to do your stuff, so get on with it."

"I think you're going about this all wrong," Cal Rivers said to the bowlegged man who barely reached to shoulder height next to his own six foot two. "How would you feel if some man came along and threw you into a cold, sterile room with a total stranger and told you to get to it, then stood by watching?"

Chaney dragged a bright red bandanna from his pocket and wiped the sweat off his leathery face. He grinned. "At my age, I'd be damned glad of the chance. 'Cept for the watching, of course. I don't go in for none of that kinky stuff.''

Cal laughed. "Come to think of it, you probably would, you old reprobate. Your courting technique doesn't seem to appeal to your four-legged friend, though."

"Son, I know more about what appeals to horse-flesh than you will if you stick around here for the next forty years. Devil's Magic is as ornery and cussed as they come. Ain't a danged thing I can do if this critter's got it into his head to take the day off."

He glared at the huge black horse in disgust. "Ain't a stallion in that barn I don't understand, 'cept for this one. If you ask me, winning all them races went to his head. Even that highfalutin stud you brought back from England ain't as difficult as he is."

A faintly critical *meow* sounded from the corner, where a fat marmalade cat regarded them haughtily. Wherever Devil's Magic went, that cat was sure to be close by. According to Chaney, the only way to get the horse into a trailer was to send the cat in ahead. At the sound of yet another meow, Devil's Magic's ears pricked up. As if he'd been waiting for a cue, he suddenly turned his attention to business. It appeared that the mare was just what he'd been looking for all his life, after all. With any luck, Mrs. Henry Robert Dolan's prized Thoroughbred mare would catch and eleven months from now would drop a foal sired by one of the biggest money winners in Florida racing history.

It went against Cal's grain to stand by and watch Chaney do most of the work, but owning a horse-breeding operation was still new to him. He'd been raised in Texas, but about as far from horses as a man could get. The lack of knowledge wasn't something that worried him, though. As he had with every business he'd ever bought he'd hired himself one of the best men he could find to run it with him. Chaney Jackson had a reputation as an intuitive, no-nonsense manager. He had set ideas about everything from feed to barn design, ideas his previous boss hadn't given him the rein or money to implement. Cal was giving him both, and they'd improved both the buildings and the paddocks so much within the first three months that owners had been quick to move horses into the new barns.

Once he'd taken care of the facilities, Cal had plunged into learning everything he could about Thoroughbred breeding and pedigrees, going straight back to the introduction of Arabian stock into England. *The General Stud Book* had become his bible. From the first, he was anticipating that day down the road when he'd have a string of the finest Thorough-bred stallions standing at stud. Devil's Magic was at the center of his plans. If everything came together as he expected, by then the business would be ripe for a takeover and he would be bored again.

It never took long for the restlessness to settle in. He was a quick learner and an instinctive entrepreneur. If he'd had more patience and more ambition, he'd be a billionaire by now, head of some international conglomerate and regularly quoted on the front page of the *Wall Street Journal*. Instead he'd been willing to settle for knowing that he had a few million in the bank, give or take the money he'd set aside to get Silver River Stables on its feet. It was more than enough to give him his freedom whenever he chose to take it.

"Why'd you buy this place anyway?" Chaney asked later that night, when they'd settled down on the porch of the graceful farmhouse that sat amidst acres of some of the most beautiful horse country in Ocala, Florida. The night air was cool and rich with the scent of grass and horses, faintly reminiscent of some of those special days in his youth when his father had let him go along with him on fruitless, humiliating job-hunting trips to ranches across Texas, ranches owned by men in the oil business who hadn't lost their shirts the way Cal's daddy had.

"You don't know a danged thing about horses, that's for sure," Chaney added with the bluntness Cal had come to admire. It was the first time, though, the older man had let himself ask a personal question, though Cal had no doubt at all the question had been nagging at him for months now. "All them books and magazines you read don't make up for doing. Did you ever see a horse up close before you signed the papers to take over here?"

Cal sipped on a beer and stared into the dwindling light as he considered the truth of Chaney's statement and his understandable bafflement. He supposed his decision to buy a Thoroughbred stud farm did seem odd to a man like Chaney who'd spent his whole life around horses and understood that world the way Cal knew about investing and making money. Unfortunately he didn't have an answer that made much sense. He'd been drawn to this place the first time he'd seen it. He hadn't been able to explain it then and he still couldn't. He settled for evasion.

"I picked a winner once at Santa Anita," he said. "A real long shot. Paid pretty decent money. I guess I got hooked."

Chaney snorted with disgust. "Big deal. I've picked a bundle of surefire winners. Don't have to mean I know diddly about breeding."

"But you do," Cal noted matter-of-factly.

"I do, indeed."

"Which is why I need you."

"That's the danged truth. I still don't get it, though. This operation didn't come cheap, even the way they'd been lettin' it go. If you got enough money to buy this place and that new stallion you picked up over in England, you could do just about anything you wanted to. There's things a whole lot less risky than breeding race horses."

"And I've already done most of 'em," Cal said. "Every one of them required that I sit indoors all day long. No matter what the business, it was getting to be dull and predictable. I was driving around out here one day, thinking about the future, when I saw this place was for sale. I decided a good risk was just what I was looking for."

Even in the shadowy light, Cal could see Chaney's disbelieving expression. "Just like that? You bought a whole danged farm just like that?"

"Just like that." It hadn't been quite that simple, of course, but pretty darned close. It had taken days of cutthroat negotiations, and even then his accountant had very nearly had apoplexy. If Joshua hadn't been his closest friend, he'd have fired him. Instead he'd tolerated the nonstop arguments, then ignored them. Joshua still refused to set foot on the farm, preferring to mutter his comments about follies and mule-headedness via long-distance.

The ability to make decisions that seemed whimsical and impractical to others was one of the few real pleasures his wealth gave him. Maybe too much thinking would have made him overly cautious, would have kept him from the riskier ventures, which were often the ones that proved to be the most exciting challenges. He wasn't much into introspection, but one thing he knew about himself: he did dearly love a challenge. Once the challenge faded, he knew it was time to move on.

Chaney rocked, staring thoughtfully toward the horizon. Cal waited, rocking rhythmically beside him and wondering why he'd never realized before that endless peace and quiet didn't necessarily equate with boredom. If he'd had to analyze the way he felt right now, he would have said he was contented. It surprised him. Contentment wasn't a state of mind with which he was all that familiar.

"A man like you, impulsive and all," Chaney began, giving him a curious, sideways glance. "You must get yourself into a hell of a mess with women."

Cal chuckled at the understatement. Whole gossip columns from Dallas to New York had been devoted to *that* subject. "I've been known to, my friend. I've been known to." There wasn't a whit of regret in his tone, though sometimes in the darkest hours of the night he had a few.

The old man's gaze narrowed, and the rocking chair creaked to a stop. "You ain't gonna have some woman coming chasing after you here, are you? Not that it's any of my business, of course, but I'm not crazy about working at a place where some woman's fussin' and changin' everything. Old man Courtney and I, we did okay here the last few years. Can't say I was happy about the way he let business slide after his wife died, but we settled into our routine. I kinda got used to the way things were with just us menfolk around, you know what I mean?"

"I know, and that's definitely not something you need to worry about," Cal promised, thinking of just how good he was getting to be at severing ties. He was thirty-seven now, and he'd had twenty years of practice. There was no one looking for him and, sadly he supposed, no one he regretted leaving behind.

"When I move on," he assured Chaney, "I never leave a forwarding address. Keeps life a whole lot less complicated."

Chapter Two

It took Marilou Stockton exactly three days, four hours and twenty-seven minutes to trace Cal Rivers to the newly named and recently renovated Silver River Stables in Ocala. She would have found him sooner if she hadn't taken time out between phone calls to sit on the sand under a palm tree for the first two days of her month-long Florida vacation. Those few hours in the sun had slowed her investigation down, but they'd definitely been worth it.

For the first time ever, her fair skin was developing a nice golden glow and, best of all, she could breathe again. She actually felt healthy instead of water-logged, which meant it was time to take care of business. Once that was done, she could really get into some serious relaxing. The anticipation of day after leisurely day under these clear tropical skies made her hurry.

She gulped down her large glass of fresh-squeezed Florida orange juice and toast, sacrificing her lazy walk on the beach in favor of studying her maps and the directions she'd been given by Cal Rivers' Palm Lane mail carrier. The carrier had turned out to be a woman in her twenties with a long memory and a talkative nature. She'd revealed that there'd been no forwarding address. Instead the mail was initially picked up weekly from the post office by a Mr. Joshua Ames, who'd had some sort of power of attorney. The mail had long since stopped coming, though, and so had this Mr. Ames.

"Too bad, too," Priscilla reported to Marilou. "He was a real hunk."

Since she didn't go to see him, Marilou couldn't attest to the man's physical attributes, but she could swear that he was about as talkative as one of those monks who'd taken a vow of silence. The instant she'd mentioned Cal Rivers on the phone, he'd clammed right up. She wondered what a man had to pay for that kind of loyalty. The only thing she'd managed to extract was an unwitting admission that Cal Rivers was still in Florida.

Which meant that he probably had a Florida driver's license.

Which meant that with a little resourcefulness—Priscilla had an old boyfriend who was a cop—Marilou was able to get his new address from the Division of Motor Vehicles. Once she had that, Priscilla had been more than happy to help her figure out the best route to take to Ocala.

By 9:00 a.m. on the fourth day of her vacation, with a renewed spirit of optimism, she was in her rental car and headed for Ocala. She figured it would take her three hours, four at the most, to actually meet Cal Rivers, senior face-to-face, hand over the letter for Cal Rivers, junior and be on her way back to the beach.

For the most part her calculations were accurate. The drive took exactly two and a half hours through terrain that changed from sand and palm trees to fields of green shaded by moss-draped oaks. She was so caught up in the dramatic shift from beach resort clutter to open spaces and Southern-style architecture that she missed the entrance to Silver River Stables and wound up going several fascinating miles out of her way. By the time she figured it out, she'd wasted nearly half an hour. In retrospect, she realized it was probably an omen.

Armed with more precise directions from a chatty gas station attendant, she finally found the discreetly marked gate. As she drove through, she noted wryly that the postal box was crammed so full of junk mail it was spilling onto the ground. Apparently this Mr. Cal Rivers had a thing about the mail. She ought to cart the whole batch up to him and dump it in his lap.

Then, again, *that* mail wasn't her worry. The letter in her purse was the only one she was here to deliver, and the sooner she did that and got on with the rest of her vacation, the better she'd like it. If she hurried, she could still be back under that palm tree with a piña colada by midafternoon. With any luck, there was still time for an adventure or two before she went back to her humdrum life in Atlanta.

Marilou parked her car in the vast shade of a sprawling live oak. As she walked toward the house, she noted the fresh coat of paint, the geranium-red trim and the sweeping veranda with a couple of well-used rockers facing west. There was something comfortable and cared-for about the house that reassured her about Cal Rivers, until she spotted the row of empty beer bottles lined up along the railing. She hadn't considered the possibility that the man might be an old drunk, an itinerant drifting from town to town only one step ahead of the law. Maybe that was why he'd vanished from Palm Lane and taken such care to cover his tracks. Her hand poised to knock, she hesitated for an instant, her gaze fastened on those bottles.

"Lady, this here's private property," growled a voice as rusty as an unoiled gate hinge. Marilou whirled around and found an old man dressed in dusty jeans and a well-worn, Western-style shirt. He regarded her suspiciously. "Whatever you're selling we don't want any."

"I'm not selling anything. I'm looking for a Mr. Cal Rivers and his little boy." She smiled. He kept right on glaring.

"Ain't no little boys around here."

"What about Mr. Rivers? Is that you?"

"Nope."

"Is he here?"

His gaze narrowed. "What do you want with him?"

She could be every bit as discreet as Joshua Ames. She said primly, "My business with Mr. Rivers is personal."

The man's scowl deepened, carving ruts in his weathered complexion. Finally he muttered something about knowing it was too good to be true, shoved a battered cap back on his head and stomped off, stirring up a trail of dust. She had no idea if he was going to get Cal Rivers or simply abandoning her here. Just as she was about to go off after him, she heard his voice again.

"I'm telling you I don't know what she wants, boss. She wouldn't tell me a danged thing. Said it was *personal*." He mimicked her tone in a way that said he knew all too well that the word meant trouble.

"Okay, Chaney, I'll take care of it," a responding voice soothed. This voice, Marilou noted with a prompt and unexpected quickening of her pulse, was low and lazy and midnight seductive. This voice promised adventure and danger in spades. She instinctively grabbed the porch rail and held on.

The man who rounded the corner of the house suited that voice. He was tall and lean, the kind of man who wore jeans and faded plaid shirts and made them look more fashionable than Armani suits. His boots, however, appeared to be every bit as new as the paint on the house. The incongruity intrigued her. She studied him more closely, trying her best not to stare with her mouth agape. The man was gorgeous, especially to someone to whom the dark, brooding type appealed.

There was a faint hint of Indian ancestry in his coal-black hair and angled features, but it had been tempered along the way. His eyes were a startling, clear blue, and right now they were as cool and distant as a mountain lake hidden amidst pine shadows. He would make a fascinating subject, she thought at once, longing for her camera.

"I understand you're looking for me," he said, stopping several yards shy of the porch steps. His expression was wary, his stance forbidding. A less determined woman than Marilou would have taken the hint and scooted right back down the steps and out of his life. Marilou squared her shoulders and smiled, relieved when his features softened ever so slightly. However slight, it was an improvement over the old man's wary antagonism.

"If you're Mr. Cal Rivers, I am," she said.

He nodded, but said nothing to invite further conversation. Southern hospitality, she thought, must stop at the Georgia border. Still, she plunged on.

"Do you have a son?"

"Nope."

The single word, confirming what she'd already been told, left absolutely no room for doubt. She supposed he certainly ought to know, but it took her aback. "Oh," she murmured, trying to readjust her thinking.

He grinned at her sudden confusion. "Am I supposed to?"

"Well, yes," she said, a little awed by the transformation of his harsh features that went with that slow, lazy grin. The devil in that smile could lure a saint to sin. With her inexperience, she'd be no match for it at all. Still, it would be a challenge to capture those quicksilver changes of mood on film. "At least, I thought you would have a son. Maybe the letter's meant for you instead."

"What letter?"

There was more wariness than curiosity behind the question, which made her increasingly nervous. She hadn't expected to feel as if she had to prove something, when she was just out to do a good deed. "The one I found," she began determinedly. "I work for the post office, you see. The dead letter office in Atlanta, actually. Well, it's a long story and—"

Suddenly her voice seemed to dry right up under his intense scrutiny. The full force of all that masculine attention was something new and decidedly disconcerting. She found herself rambling, despite her parched throat. "I'm very thirsty. The drive was longer than I expected and I didn't want to take the time to stop. Then I got lost. Do you suppose I could have a glass of water or something before I tell you the rest?"

"Chaney," Cal said curtly. The little man who'd been hovering in the background stomped off toward the back of the house. He was muttering under his breath again.

"He doesn't seem to like visitors," she observed.

"Chaney is highly suspicious of women who have personal business with me. He figures it'll disrupt the routine around here. Judging from the last few minutes, I'd say he's very astute."

Marilou recognized a criticism when she heard it, but if he'd intended to chase her off with his sharp tongue and cool manner it was just too bad. When she didn't budge, he said grudgingly, "I suppose you might as well sit until Chaney gets back. You look as if you've spent too much time in the sun."

So much for her tan, she thought ruefully.

Taking his grudging offer at face value, Marilou chose the rocker that was farthest from the beer bottles. His gaze followed her, but he didn't say a word. The silence, coupled with the thoroughness of his scrutiny, was definitely unnerving. Men didn't usually look at her like that, as if she were mysterious and fascinating and dangerous. She supposed it made sense in this instance. After all, she had popped up here out of the blue and she still hadn't explained why she'd come. No wonder the man was staring. It probably wasn't a bit personal. That realization didn't stop the fluttering of her pulse, though. With his gaze steady on her, it felt personal. When Chaney came back with a tall glass of ice-cold lemonade, she clung to it, taking a deep swallow. Maybe she wasn't cut out for adventure after all, not if it involved blatantly masculine men like Cal Rivers.

"As I was saying," she began, rushing now, wanting this over with. "The other day I got this letter. It had been sent to the wrong address. Palm Tree Lane instead of Palm Lane. I suppose it was a simple enough mistake to make. I still think the mail carrier should have been able to figure it out, but Priscilla says it must have come through on her day off.''

''Priscilla?''

''Your old mail carrier. Anyway, the letter wound up in Atlanta, because there wasn't any return address, either. That's what happens when a letter goes astray. It comes to me, or actually to my branch. I guess I should have thrown it out, but I just couldn't. She sounded so pitiful, you see. I...''

''Slow down,'' Cal advised, unexpected amusement again lurking in the depths of his eyes. ''This isn't an emergency.''

''But it could be,'' she insisted. ''I mean the letter says she's dying.''

Cal looked startled. Even Chaney seemed taken aback by her announcement. ''Who's dying?'' Cal demanded. ''What the devil are you talking about, woman?''

''I'm sorry. I should have said right away. It's your grandmother.''

The words had an incredible effect. His expression, which had been gently tolerant only an instant before, froze into icy disdain. ''You have the wrong person,'' he said, turning his back on her. The muscles across his shoulders tensed visibly.

''No, I don't think so,'' she said stubbornly, ignoring his reaction. ''You did live on Palm Lane, didn't you?''

When he didn't answer, she got up and moved until she was standing in his line of vision again. "Didn't you?" she demanded, catching the brief flash of confusion in his eyes before he shut off any evidence of emotion again.

"Yes," he said finally.

"Then, see," she coaxed reasonably, "it has to be you."

"I'm telling you that I am not the man you're looking for."

Marilou lost patience with him. How could anyone be so stubborn and ornery in the face of the evidence? "I don't know how you can say that, unless you figure that there was another Cal Rivers living in that very house."

"Lady, I do not have a grandmother." His voice rose to a defiant roar that carried on the still air.

"Of course you do," she said impatiently. "Everyone has grandparents."

"Mine are dead," he declared with absolutely no emotion. "Gone. I've never met any of them."

"But that's just it," she said excitedly. "Something happened a long time ago. I don't know what exactly, but she's sorry. Maybe everyone thought it would be better if you just thought she was dead. At any rate, she really wants to make it up to you, and she's dying. If you don't hurry, it might be too late."

"I'm very sorry that this lady, whoever she is, is dying, but it has nothing to do with me."

Sensing that she was losing, and desperate not to, Marilou took a few steps forward until she was practically toe-to-toe with him. He looked miserable and uncomfortable, but he didn't back up when she told him, "It has everything to do with you. Please, you have to see that."

Cal tried to stare her down, and when that didn't work, he demanded, "What is this woman's name?"

"I . . . I don't know. It wasn't on the letter."

"Then how can you possibly be so certain she's a relative of mine? Do you think you know more about my family than I do?"

"No, but the letter was addressed to you."

"Where does this woman live?"

"In Wyoming. I don't know exactly where. It was postmarked Cheyenne, but it could have come from anywhere around there, I suppose. Mail from a lot of small towns winds up being postmarked from the nearest big city. There wasn't any street address. That's why I couldn't send the letter back to her."

Even though his anger was daunting, Marilou was watching his face closely. She saw the faint flicker of recognition, when she'd mentioned Wyoming. "I'm right, aren't I? You did have relatives in Wyoming, didn't you?"

He gazed off in the distance. "A long time ago, maybe. I don't know," he said, his tone distracted. Then his expression turned fierce again. "I think you'd better leave."

This wasn't going at all the way she'd anticipated. She felt tears beginning to well up in her eyes and re-alized she was going to make an even bigger fool of herself by crying. "I can't," she replied softly. "I have to see this through."

"You have seen it through," he countered impatiently. "You've done your job. I'm sure the post office will give you your bonus or whatever."

Marilou was thoroughly insulted that he thought that's what this was all about. "The post office doesn't even know I'm here. If they did, they'd probably fire me."

He stared at her. "What are you saying?"

"I took a vacation to find you."

"Well, I'll be," Chaney muttered, his expression totally agog.

Cal paced, shaking his head. Finally he turned. "Lady, are you nuts?" His tone was suddenly more bemused than furious.

"No, I am not nuts," she said defensively. "I just happen to care about this."

"Why? Is there some sort of reward for meddling in things that are none of your concern? I'll see that you get it."

"Dammit, this has nothing to do with any reward. It's about family. What's more important than that?"

"Money," he said so promptly it made her blood run cold. He meant it, too. She could tell that. Nothing she was saying about his grandmother seemed to be penetrating that thick skull of his. It was disappointing that a man this gorgeous had to be such an idiot.

Ignoring him, she sank back down in the rocker to think. What the dickens was she supposed to do now?

She had thought it was going to be a simple matter of finding Cal Rivers, explaining about the letter and then walking away. Instead she was faced with a man who wouldn't even believe that he had a grandmother and, worse, didn't seem to care one way or the other.

No, she corrected. That wasn't quite true. There had been that one brief second when he'd revealed a hint of vulnerability, a moment of confusion. Maybe he was afraid for some reason. She studied the unyielding set of his shoulders, the angry scowl on his face. He didn't look like the sort to be scared of anything short of a raging stampede of horses. More likely, he was an insensitive, uncaring jerk. Not everyone had good in them, despite what she'd been taught.

She ought to leave and let him stay here and get snockered on beer every night. Maybe the beer helped him to live with whatever had made him the cold, uncaring man that he was. It certainly wasn't up to her to reform him. There probably weren't enough years left in her lifetime to accomplish that.

Then she thought of the letter in her purse. She owed it to that dear old lady to try harder. Cal Rivers might not be much by her standards, but he was family. And Marilou was the only hope either of them had, the only link. There was an old saying about fools rushing in. Well, she'd already rushed. She might as well stick around for the consequences. If she sat her for a little while, surely something would come to her.

Besides, as she debated whether to go or stay, the clouds had begun building in the west. Fat drops of rain were already plopping into the dust. She re-

garded the sudden downpour with a sense of resignation. There was apparently no escape anywhere from
these damn April showers.

"I don't think she's planning on leavin', boss,"
Chaney said, his baleful gaze resting on the pretty little redhead who'd plunked herself down in a chair on
the porch and was rocking to beat the band.

Cal didn't think she was going anywhere either. He
noted the stubborn set of her chin and the fire in her
green eyes and decided he might have miscalculated
just the tiniest bit about the pesky woman with her
crazy story about a dying grandmother. It wouldn't be
the first time some reporter or gold-digger had used an
outrageous tale to get to him. This one was better than
most. He'd give her that. She almost had him believ-
ing her.

She was also the most stubborn female he'd encountered in some time. He'd attempted to brush her
off with a chilly reception and a few intimidating
words. Obviously, it was going to take more. He just
wasn't quite sure what would work with a woman who
was apparently so dead-sure she was on a mission.
Maybe he could cajole her into going with a promise
or two. It wouldn't kill him to fib a little, if it meant
dislodging her from that chair and his life.

"Okay," he said at last, willing himself to look
cooperative. "I'm not saying I believe you, but I'm
willing to look into it. Leave the letter with me and I'll
check it out."

The expression she directed at him was very wary. "Check it out how?"

Her persistence almost cost him the tight rein on his temper. "I'll have to think about it. Maybe I'll hire a private investigator. Yes," he said, warming up to the notion. She ought to buy that. "I'll hire a detective."

She was shaking her head. "That's a waste of perfectly good money. I can find her for you in no time and I won't charge you a penny."

"Really," he protested desperately. "That's not necessary. I can afford it and I really can't take up any more of your time."

Her gaze narrowed suspiciously. "You're just trying to get rid of me, aren't you? You figure I'll give you the letter and walk out and you'll tear it up the minute my back is turned."

"Lady, if you're so dead-set sure that the letter is mine, then what I do with it is none of your business."

She frowned at him, her expression thoughtful. "I suppose you're right."

"Of course I am. You've done all you can do. You can go now and your conscience will be perfectly clear."

She nodded slowly and his mood brightened considerably. Then she turned one of those penetrating looks on him, a look that seemed to see straight into his lying heart. "Nope. I can't do that," she said, sounding downright sorrowful. "I feel responsible."

Cal lost his last thread of restraint. "Dammit, you are not responsible!"

"I can't help how I feel."

"Feel any way you want to, just do it someplace else."

"Let me just make a few calls for you, get the search started."

"No!"

"It'll relieve my mind."

"No!"

She nodded, her expression triumphant. "I knew you weren't really going to follow through."

Cal threw up his hands in a gesture of defeat. "That's it. I give up."

He was no more than half a dozen feet from the porch, when Chaney stopped him. "What should I do about her?" he asked, gazing pointedly toward Marilou.

"Ignore her," Cal said finally, stalking off into the rain. "I'm going back to Lady Mary."

As an interim plan, it would have to do, but he had no doubt it wouldn't be the end of Miss Marilou Stockton. Oh, she looked like a frail little thing with her sunburned nose and too-big T-shirt. In fact, for an instant there he'd been drawn to her innocence and naiveté. It was a knee-jerk reaction to a woman who looked as if she needed protecting. Fortunately he'd learned long ago that those kind of women were the most dangerous of all. They usually had a streak of muleheadedness that drove a man nuts. So far, Marilou was running true to form. She'd be waiting whenever he decided to come back. He had no doubts about that.

"I'm going to strangle Joshua the next time I see him," he muttered. The accountant had to be behind this visit. No one else could have pointed the way from his last address to this place. Joshua was probably sitting in that fancy office of his chortling with glee this very minute. He no doubt considered it just revenge for Cal's failure to heed his advice.

Hell, for all he knew Joshua had made up the damned letter in the first place. He'd been making less than subtle noises about it being time for a family reunion for months now, preaching a lot of psychological hogwash about facing the past. The more Cal thought about it, the more sense it made. Joshua was definitely behind this visit.

Disgusted at the abrupt end to his new-found peace and quiet and unable to think of a single tactic to rid himself permanently of his unwanted visitor, Cal ignored the downpour and headed for the barn. He might not know much about horses, but he figured he had a better shot at understanding them than he ever would figuring out women or friends who meddled in things that were none of their business.

He'd left Zeke walking Lady Mary and the groom could probably use someone to spell him. From what Chaney'd taught him colic in a horse was nothing to fool around with. If the mare hadn't improved, he'd probably have the vet out before the night was over. Lady Mary's health was a helluva lot more important than listening to this woman's crazy tales.

Before he turned the corner toward the stables, though, he made the mistake of casting one last look over his shoulder. Marilou's rocker had gone perfectly still. She was staring after him, an expression of stunned indignation on her face. Even Chaney looked startled by the abrupt dismissal. He was staring worriedly from Cal to their unwanted guest and back again. Cal glared back at both of them. He had nothing to apologize for. If he didn't want anybody dredging up his past, that was his business, right? Damn right!

So why was there this incredibly guilty knot in his gut, a knot that was probably every bit as painful as Lady Mary's colic?

Chapter Three

Marilou did not consider herself to be either an especially assertive woman or a femme fatale type, but few men had ever had the audacity to flat-out ignore her. None that she could recall had ever walked off in the middle of an argument. It took her fully sixty seconds to recuperate from the shock of watching Cal Rivers deliver the last word then turn his back on her and go charging off to see this Lady Mary, whoever she was.

The image of rough and rowdy Cal Rivers with some elegant member of the British aristocracy seemed ludicrous to her. Now an Irish barmaid, that was something else. She could envision that all too clearly. Unexpected jealousy taunted her.

Startled by the absurdly out of place and purely feminine reaction, she looked up to find Chaney watching her. Fortunately he didn't appear to have picked up on her thoughts. Instead he seemed torn with indecision. Finally he shrugged half-apologetically and started off in the same direction Cal had taken. He was partway across the yard before he turned with obvious reluctance and came back.

"You might's well take off," he said. He sounded hopeful.

Unwilling to accept defeat, Marilou shook her head. "I don't think so. Not until he promises to follow up on his grandmother's letter."

Chaney squinted at her curiously, his action emphasizing the deep furrows in his tanned brow. "You ain't family, are you?"

"No."

"You ever met him before?"

"No."

"You one of them paid do-gooders? Like a social worker or some such?"

"I told you. I work for the post office and I'm not even here in an official capacity."

"Then I just don't get it. What difference does it make to you what he does?"

"His grandmother is dying," she repeated, incredulous at his lack of understanding. Was she the only one left in the world who cared about family?

"This might be their only chance to meet and reconcile. Doesn't that matter to you?" she demanded.

"You could help, you know. Maybe he'd listen to you."

Chaney shuffled and looked uncomfortable. He slapped his hat against his thigh, then shoved it back on his head. Staring at his feet, he mumbled, "Ain't no reason I can see for me to get involved. The world would be a whole lot better off if more people just minded their own business. Hell, I don't even know the woman."

"But . . ."

He persisted. "Apparently he don't know her either."

"Then it's about time he did, before it's too late and he has to deal with a whole lot of guilt."

Chaney seemed to get a big kick out of that idea. "I ain't known him all that long, but I don't think Cal Rivers is the kind of man to be much troubled by guilt."

"More's the pity."

Chaney's mouth gaped at the sarcasm. Obviously he considered Cal Rivers' behavior to be above reproach. "Okay," he said finally, "so let's just say that you ain't going till he agrees to this." He regarded her now with open curiosity. "How you gonna talk him into it?"

Marilou frowned and admitted, "If I knew that, I'd be out there after him instead of wasting my vacation in this chair. I'll think of something, though. I can promise you that."

"Maybe you ought to go think on it someplace else. He sees you here later, he's likely to be madder than an old wet hen. He ain't the kind of man who likes to be pushed.''

"What kind of man is he?" she asked, seizing the opening and hoping for clues that would help her plot a new strategy.

"One who wouldn't like me gossiping about him."

"It wouldn't be gossip," she said. At the lift of Chaney's bushy gray brows, she added, "Not exactly."

"You put whatever name you like on it, I ain't saying a thing. He owns this place, and I'd like to hang on to my job."

"So, he's tough."

"Listen here, missy, you didn't hear me say nothing like that."

She grinned innocently. "I could have sworn I did."

"Women!" He threw up his hands in disgust. "You just go on and think what you like. I'll be getting back to work now."

"Thanks for the talk."

"We didn't have no talk. If you say we did, I'll call you a liar."

"I suspect your boss is already calling me far worse," she said, surprised by the odd little pang of regret that crept through her. Why should it bother her what a jerk thought?

Chaney muttered something unintelligible, then said grudgingly, "If you want any more of that lemonade, there's a pitcher full in the refrigerator. I suppose you might's well help yourself."

"Thanks." Surprised by the gesture, she nodded. She considered whether it would be wise to probe any more, then decided to risk the one question that had been nagging at her. She knew that the old hand could answer it, if he was of a mind to.

"Chaney?"

"Ma'am?"

"Who's Lady Mary? Would she have any influence with him?" She tried to inject the question with nothing more than innocent curiosity, but it seemed to reverberate with hidden meanings. Maybe a man wouldn't notice them, she thought hopefully.

Chaney obviously did. She caught the faint suggestion of a sly smile tugging at his usually sour, down-turned mouth. "Why, ma'am, I'm not so sure that's something I ought to be discussing with you," he said evasively. "I suppose if you get real curious, sooner or later you'll find out for yourself."

Marilou had a feeling that there was the tiniest suggestion of implied criticism in his comment, but there was also a dare. Somehow she knew that before the day was out, she'd take him up on it.

Once she'd been left on her own, Marilou decided that a little more lemonade might help her quench this odd, insatiable thirst that had developed the minute she had laid eyes on Cal Rivers with his gray-blue eyes, pitch-black hair and powerful masculine body that belonged astride a horse.

Or a woman.

Dear heavens, where had that wayward thought come from? Foolish question. The man's sex appeal was practically branded on him. He radiated sexual energy the way Florida Power and Light sent out electricity. It was just what they did. That didn't mean she had to fall under his spell. She refused to behave that predictably.

She hurriedly poured herself another glass of the thirst-quenching lemonade, then wandered into the living room, looking around with blatant curiosity at the prissy furniture that didn't fit at all the man she'd just met. It must have come with the house, or else this Lady Mary had done the decorating with all the dark wood and old-fashioned brocades. She wandered on, poking her head into other rooms as she went. Snooping, her mother would have said disapprovingly. Marilou preferred to think of it as reconnaissance. She needed to know everything she could about Cal Rivers if she was going to talk him into doing what was right.

"You know I'm right about this, Mama," she murmured aloud, just in case her mother was someplace where she could see her.

Admittedly she was finding her survey fascinating. Cal's office, when she discovered it, was more what she'd expected. With its worn leather furniture and fox hunt prints, it looked comfortable and well-used, exactly like the kind of place a single man would choose to spend a quiet evening. There was even an old stonehearth fireplace that would be just right on one of Central Florida's chilly winter nights. There was another row of empty beer bottles on the window sill behind the huge oak desk. Magazines were scattered helter-skelter on the hardwood floor, an incongruous mix of business publications and farm magazines plus some days-old copies of the *Racing Form*. Shirts had been tossed over the backs of chairs...and forgotten, judging from the barnyard smell of them.

Psychologically incapable of remaining idle for long, Marilou stacked the magazines by topic, dumped the beer bottles into the trash can, then gathered up the shirts and carried them into the kitchen in search of a washing machine. It occurred to her as she tossed them into the brand-new automatic washer that she was overstepping Chaney's hospitality.

Overstepping, hell. These were giant strides, she thought with a twinge of conscience.

Still, maybe they'd both be so grateful to have clean shirts they wouldn't complain. Then she recalled the hard expression in Cal's eyes just before he'd stalked off. He'd label it meddling and she knew it. Gratitude would probably be the last thing on his mind. She'd be lucky if he didn't have her charged with breaking and entering and then hauled off to jail. Now that would be an adventure.

Even at the risk of incurring his wrath, though, she had to keep busy. She always thought better when her hands were occupied, and right now she needed to think of a compelling argument to convince Cal to go see his grandmother. Frankly, though, she couldn't imagine anything much more important than the woman's impending death. What kind of hard-hearted creature could ignore that?

She paused, the cup of detergent suspended over the washer and recalled their conversation from start to finish. For just a heartbeat, she could have sworn she'd seen something vulnerable in those cool-as-gunmetal eyes of his. If only she could reach that part of him again, make him see that it was time to let bygones be bygones. He had a gentle, thoughtful side. She was sure of it.

"What the hell do you think you're doing?"

The furious voice whipped across her. She spun around, scattering blue powder in every direction, and met an icy glare. She would have given almost anything for a hint of that vulnerability now, but all she saw was steel and fury. He looked hard and deepdown angry and, try as she might, she couldn't really say she blamed him.

"I'm sorry," she said at once. "I was thinking and when I think I need to be doing something and it looked as if there was a lot around here that needed doing so I just . . . I just sort of did it. I'm sorry."

Cal poked his thumbs through the waistband of his jeans and swore softly. "Chaney was right. You're not going to give up, are you?"

Marilou gave the rhetorical question all the consideration he expected and answered right back, "Probably not."

His gaze narrowed. "Did Joshua send you here?"

"Joshua? Oh, you mean Mr. Ames." She grinned. "We talked."

"And he told you how to find me. I knew it!"

"Not exactly. If you're paying him to keep his mouth shut, he's living up to his end of the bargain."

"Then how?"

"I can be very resourceful when I have to be. He dropped a couple of clues, unwittingly by the way, and I ran with them. Don't go blaming him for my turning up here."

He raked his fingers through his hair. "Dammit all to hell, woman, what is it you want from me?"

"It's not all that complicated. I just want you to go see your grandmother. If you'd just read the letter, you'd see how important it is." She reached in her pocket for the envelope, but he was already backing away as if she were about to offer him a red-hot poker, fiery end first.

"It's just a letter, for goodness sakes. It wouldn't kill you to read it."

"How do I even know she's mine?"

The look Marilou gave him when he said that would have withered a cactus. Cal muttered another oath under his breath and realized he'd done more swearing in the past few hours than he'd done in the past year. It was not a good sign. He only cussed when he couldn't think of anything sensible to say. This pint-size hellion did not inspire clear thinking. Between needling his conscience and triggering his hormones, she was more worrisome than a boardroom filled with outraged stockholders. He knew how to soothe them with bottom lines and profit margins. He didn't have a clue about what tactics might work on the woman whose big green eyes were fixed on him so steadily. He hated the disappointment that rose in them every time he denied this grandmother she claimed was his.

"Okay," he said finally. "You say she's mine. I asked before and I'll say it again: How come nobody in my family ever mentioned her?"

"Did you ask?"

Cal squirmed under that direct, no-nonsense gaze. He wondered if this prickly woman had a husband. Despite her obvious physical attributes, he couldn't imagine any man in his right mind putting up with her. She'd be hell on a guilty conscience. She was playing havoc with his, and he didn't have a blasted thing to feel guilty about. He'd put his family ties, such as they were, behind him long ago to no one's regret.

"No, I never asked. I figured you either had grandparents or you didn't. If you didn't, most likely they were dead."

"Well, one of yours isn't. Yet," she amended significantly.

"Okay. Okay. You've made your point. I'll think about what you've said. Go on back to wherever you came from and I'll take care of it."

If he expected that to be the end of it, he quickly realized that he'd underestimated her determination. She regarded him with blatant skepticism. "That doesn't sound like much of a promise to me. How do I know you won't rip up the letter the minute I'm out the door?"

"You don't."

He knew it was the wrong answer the minute he'd said it. He cursed himself for a fool when she scowled, folded her arms across her chest and declared with open defiance, "Then I'm not going."

"Good Lord, woman, do you plan to move in?"

That took a little of the starch out of her. She struck him as the sort of woman who jumped in impetuously and then was too stubborn to back down. Once she saw the obvious implications of her crazy stance, she'd run. Never in a million years would she allow herself to be trapped into staying with a couple of men she'd never seen before today. She'd be on the road by sundown and glad to escape.

"No, of course not...I mean..."

There, he thought with satisfaction, grinning at her confusion. "Puts you in a bit of a quandary then, doesn't it?"

Her gaze narrowed at the ill-advised taunt, and her chin rose another notch. "Maybe I will, after all...if that's what it takes."

It was sheer bravado, but Cal had been in enough negotiating sessions in his time to recognize a tactical blunder when it smacked him between the eyes. He'd pushed too hard...again. He should have given her room to maneuver, to retreat gracefully. He found an out and offered it, a little desperately if the truth be known. "You're probably expected back at your hotel."

"No," she said, too quickly, then reconsidered. "I mean, not for hours yet."

He threw up his hands at her naïveté. A woman this innocent had no business being let loose on her own. "Don't you know how much trouble you could get yourself into telling a strange man that you're all alone down here?'' he asked impatiently. ''You don't know anything about me. I could be a second cousin to Jack the Ripper.''

Surprisingly she grinned at his irritation. ''I doubt that.''

''You're too damned trusting.''

''Not really. I just figure that the second cousin to Jack the Ripper would not go planting the idea in my mind, unless it was meant to scare me off.''

''That's exactly what it's meant to do.''

''But not because you're dangerous,'' she said with such absolute certainty that it gave him an odd little quiver in the region of his heart. ''You just don't want to deal with this business about your grandmother.''

''Fine. You caught me. I don't want to deal with it. I am not going to deal with it. So you might as well go.''

She was shaking her head before he was done. She squared her shoulders and then she smiled. That smile had probably devastated tougher men than him. Cal fought its impact without much success. He could feel the warmth seeping into him, curling around his cold emotions.

''I don't think I'll leave just yet,'' she said softly.

Something that felt astonishingly like relief flooded through him. He suddenly realized that the prospect of having Miss Marilou Stockton around a while longer wasn't quite as displeasing as it ought to have been. Maybe he wasn't nearly as keen on peace and quiet as he'd thought.

Or maybe he'd just noticed how seeing a woman in this big old homey kitchen felt right. He wondered what other rooms she'd suit. He doubted that the feisty little gal in front of him would be flattered if she knew the decidedly wicked direction his thoughts were taking. Nor would she feel quite so safe. It would be better in the long run for both of them if she went now.

"If you're staying, how about fixing dinner?" he baited, trying a new tactic and wondering exactly how far he'd have to push her before she'd bolt from this dare. Finding out could be fascinating. Nothing entertained him more than testing the mettle of a woman. He hadn't met one yet who could withstand his scrutiny.

Ignoring the dull flush creeping into her cheeks, he added, "Chaney and I are getting tired of steak, which is about the only thing we can cook without ruining it."

"If you'd weed that garden I saw out back, maybe you'd have some decent vegetables to have with your steak."

"I'm not looking for recipes. I'm after a cook. Are you willing?"

She stared at him incredulously, clearly stunned by this unexpected turnaround. "You . . . you *want* me to stay?"

He shrugged indifferently. "Suit yourself. All I'm saying is if you're going to hang around, you might as well make yourself useful. I've been thinking it was about time to hire on a housekeeper. I suppose you'd do as good as anyone."

"I would do? *Do?*" Indignation sparked in her eyes. "You're crazy, you know that? You are flat-out, ought-to-be-locked-up crazy if you think I'm going to play housekeeper for the pair of you."

"There's no playing to it. I'll pay good wages. Besides, it looks to me as if you've already got a good start on the job," he said, gazing pointedly in the direction of the washer, which was now well into its spin cycle and apparently without the benefit of detergent, since the powder was all over the floor. "Might's well plunge in whole hog."

Her gaze narrowed. "I thought you wanted me as far away from here as possible and the sooner the better."

He grinned. It was working. At last he'd found the way to make her turn tail and run. "Maybe I've reconsidered. I'm a pragmatic man. You're still here. It's getting dark and Chaney and I are getting hungry."

"I thought you'd be eating with Lady what's-her-name."

He almost burst out laughing at that, but managed to say with a straight face, "She's a little off her feed tonight."

"Too bad." She said it politely enough, but for a woman who'd gone all mushy about his grandmother, she didn't seem to him to be very sorry for Lady Mary.

"So, how about it?" he prodded. "The refrigerator's well stocked."

"Then use your imagination and fix your own damn meal," she suggested, but she didn't bolt for the door as he'd intended. Nor did she make a move toward the stove. As a matter of fact, she pulled out a chair and plunked herself down on it, then stared up at him expectantly, those big green eyes flashing fire again. The responding heat that flamed through him took him by surprise. He suddenly realized that this latest miscalculation was likely to cost him dearly. It took her about ten seconds to confirm it.

She smiled up at him with saucy arrogance and said sweetly, "As long as you're cooking, I'll take my steak rare."

Chapter Four

Marilou was fully aware that she had just boxed herself into an impossible corner. Even as the words had tumbled across her lips, she'd been astonished at her impulsive declaration. Moving in, for heaven's sakes? Was she out of her mind or simply out of her depth?

Well, she was definitely the latter and quite possibly the former. Matching wits with a man like Cal Rivers was no game for a woman like her. She didn't have the slightest idea of the rules or how to play by them.

At some point, she had vaguely recognized the subtle shift from mental to sensual challenge, and still she'd been helpless to abandon the fray. In fact, to her shock, she'd been invigorated by it, compelled to take his dares simply because he'd made them and because she knew that he'd expected her to refuse. She'd enjoyed watching his expression go from wary to amused to stunned in a matter of seconds. It was the most exciting, reckless thing she'd done in all of her twenty-five years.

Now, with second thoughts popping up like weeds, it appeared she was stuck. She couldn't very well say thanks for the steak, then wave and wander off once dinner was done. He'd be laughing at her from now till Sunday. No, her pride wouldn't permit that. Nor would her determined commitment to Cal's grandmother, a woman she was never even likely to meet but for whom she felt an odd, special kinship. Besides, she countered the rising doubts, this might very well be the closest she ever came to a longed-for adventure. She wasn't about to walk away from it just when it was getting interesting.

Actually, it was getting downright fascinating, she decided as she gazed out the back door and watched the subtle bunching of the muscles across Cal's broad shoulders as he hunkered down to start the grill, a puny little hibachi meant for picnics, not full-scale dinners at home. He'd stuffed a package of frozen vegetables into the microwave, along with three potatoes, and turned it on for twenty minutes. Marilou shuddered. The minute he wasn't looking she retrieved the vegetables and waited expectantly for the potatoes to explode, since he hadn't bothered to pierce the skins.

Directing a glare at her as he entered, he stomped past, grabbed a package of steaks from the freezer and headed for the still-cold grill. Marilou couldn't bear to watch.

"Cal?" she said finally.

"What?" he growled.

"Don't you think you ought to defrost those first in the microwave?"

"They'll defrost on the grill."

"Not in this lifetime."

"Either you cook or you shut up. I don't need any coaching from the sidelines."

She groaned as he plunked the solid steaks onto the grill. "No. You do need a housekeeper. I can see that now. Maybe we could strike a deal after all."

He gazed at her distrustfully. "Oh?"

"Just short-term. I'll help out around here tonight, if you'll think about going to see your grandmother." She discovered that she was not above a little bribery. It was not a discovery that especially pleased her.

He regarded the icy beef, frowned, then met her gaze.

"No steaks?"

She hurriedly improvised a menu. "Spaghetti with the best sauce this side of Italy."

His expression brightened hopefully, like a kid promised chocolate chip cookies. "No kidding?"

"I never kid about my sauce."

"No more nagging, at least through dinner?"

"No nagging," she conceded reluctantly.

"You don't expect any promises?"

"No promises, except that you'll do some honest soul-searching."

"You drive a hard bargain for such a little thing, but for a decent meal I think I just might promise you the moon."

"We'll save that, in case you haven't made up your mind by breakfast."

A killer grin spread across his face, the kind of grin that made female knees go weak and hearts pound. Her body responded with disgusting predictability as he warned, "Be careful, lady. You tell me you can make pancakes and easy-over eggs and it could take me months to give this problem the thoughtful consideration it deserves."

"Oh, no," she said, laughing. "This offer has an expiration date, and it could change at any second if I suspect you're not keeping your end of the deal."

"Are you married, Marilou Stockton?"

She was startled by the question and by the fact that he'd leaned in close to ask it. She could smell the heady masculine scent of him and feel the tug of his body heat. "No," she said, her voice suddenly whisper soft.

He nodded in satisfaction, then grinned. "I didn't think so."

"Why?"

"Because you've got a tongue that's sharp enough to cut out a man's heart."

"That's a dangerous thing to say to a woman you're expecting to cook your dinner."

"You won't lace the food with arsenic."

"What makes you so sure?"

"Then you'd never get me to Wyoming." He was whistling cheerfully as he left the room, so cheerfully in fact that Marilou wondered if she hadn't just played right into his hand. The amazing thing was that she didn't seem to care if she had. She was beginning to enjoy the unexpected and thoroughly outrageous twists and turns the day had taken.

If Chaney was stunned to find Marilou in the kitchen and spaghetti with homemade sauce on the table, he kept it to himself, casting sly glances from her to his taciturn boss and back again. He attacked the dinner like a man who'd been starved, and whatever questions he had about the turn of events, he bit back, while Marilou was left with a whole string of questions herself.

Why had Cal gone to such pains to vanish from his Palm Lane home? Why did he clam up so whenever the talk turned to family? What sort of secrets had his family kept from him? Or had he been abandoned? Maybe that was why this whole discussion about a long-lost grandmother made him prickly as an old bear startled out of its winter slumber.

Whatever the case, she apparently wasn't going to be allowed to satisfy her curiosity tonight. She'd promised to cut him some slack and she would. Not that he gave her much choice. His good humor had vanished sometime between her offer to cook and his return to the table. Aside from a few surreptitious glances in her direction, he ate silently, apparently lost in his own thoughts. She could only hope they were about his grandmother. If his troubled expression was any indication, they had to be.

The minute the meal was over, Cal muttered a grudging thanks and stalked off into the night again. Chaney, with one last speculative look at Marilou, traipsed after him. Marilou was left with a huge stack of dirty dishes. And when they were done and neither of the men had reappeared, she was left with figuring out where she might sleep.

She found sheets that smelled of sunshine stacked in a closet in the upstairs hall. She grabbed a couple and began making up the bed in what appeared to be a vacant bedroom, as far from the master bedroom as she could get.

She'd seen the size of the bed in his room. Just the sight of it had done funny things to her insides. She'd made things worse by daring to test its feather softness before retreating guiltily. At the memory of the way that bed had made her feel, she felt a blush creeping into her cheeks.

Just then she heard the flick of a match and caught the scent of sulphur. Until that second she hadn't even realized that Cal had come up the stairs. A faint puff of smoke from his cigarette drifted into the room.

"You look like you're settling in," he said, his voice dropping to a lazy, seductive tone that brought goose bumps to her flesh and set off a whole new flurry of doubts about her decision to stay. Visions of that bed down the hall stirred up a storm of sensations.

"This room seemed to be empty," she said, keeping her back to him as she smoothed the pillow. "I hope it's okay."

"It's fine, though there's one down the hall you might enjoy more," he said. "I'd be happy to keep you company."

Her skin burned at the deliberately provocative invitation. "Thanks, but you probably snore."

"You'll never know till you spend the night with me."

"I could always bug your room."

He chuckled at the quick retort. "You know, most women would have been scared off by now," he said. She thought she detected a very faint and very reluctant note of admiration in his voice.

"I've told you before that you don't scare me," she responded lightly, ignoring the rapid thudding of her heart, which contradicted her words. She turned to stare directly at him just to prove the point. "You're all bluff."

There was a quick flash of amusement in his eyes before they began a low, deliberate inspection. Her pulse hammered and heat rose through her before she finally shifted her gaze away. No man's look had ever been so blatantly seductive. She would have picked up a magazine and fanned herself if he hadn't been watching. Of course, if he hadn't been watching, she wouldn't have needed to. It was just more of his game and she knew it. Her body apparently didn't.

"I wouldn't call my bluff if I were you," he warned, still not taking his eyes off of her. "You just might get

more than you bargained for, Miss Marilou Stockton. A lot more.''

After one last, lingering glance that made her knees
wobble, he walked on down the hall. Marilou sank
down on the edge of the bed and fanned herself so
hard that the magazine she was using almost came
apart in her hands. She had a feeling Cal's touch
would have the exact same effect on her senses. If she
let this man get any closer, she'd never be whole again
unless he were around to see to it. The prospect
tempted, even as it unsettled her.

In the end it was the longest, most nerve-racking
night of Marilou's life. She heard the groan of Cal's
bed, the thump of his boots hitting the floor, then
more creaking as he settled onto that feather mattress
for the night. As the cool night breeze ruffled the cur-
tains, she could swear she heard him breathing . . . but
not snoring.

She eventually drifted into a restless sleep, but at
4:00 a.m. she was awakened by some faint noise. She
listened, but all she heard now was absolute silence.
Finally she abandoned any hope of sleeping, pulled on
her clothes from the day before and crept barefoot
downstairs. After an instant's guilty hesitation in front
of the automatic coffeepot, she gave in to her need for
caffeine. She supposed for the moment she could
make a case that she was still playing housekeeper, at
least for the next few hours until she had Cal's answer.

She wondered if his response, even a positive one,
was likely to be enough for her now. Always readily

hooked by mysteries, was she going to be able to walk away from this one without knowing the ending or the secrets still hidden from her? Would she be able to forget so easily the man whose pain ran so deep that he'd chosen to shut out the world and let Joshua Ames run interference for him?

She sighed. Coffee cup in hand, she wandered outside. The air was chilly and the grass glistened with dew in the light from a full moon. She breathed deeply, entranced by the unfamiliar earthy scents. There was something raw and basic, something untouched by all the manufactured perfumes and air-conditioned sterility of the city. She stepped onto the cool carpet of lawn, feeling a childlike exhilaration as her bare feet met the dampness. Suddenly she remembered other mornings, creeping barefooted out of the house to get the paper without waking her parents, feeling as if the world was hers and hers alone at that silent hour before even the birds began to greet the dawn.

She went back inside for her shoes, then set out to explore, taking the path that Cal had taken the day before. As she turned the corner of the house, she was surprised to discover him on the track beyond the stables. Obviously the sound of his leaving had been what had awakened her. She started toward him, then stopped in the shadows to watch in wonder. All the gentleness she had suspected and that he normally worked so hard to hide was in full view now.

He was walking a horse, one hand on the lead, the other in constant motion, caressing in slow, calming strokes as they went round and round the oval track. She could hear his low crooning, the soothing tone but not the words, and realized that she envied both words and touch.

Concern washed through her as she noted that his shoulders were slumped with exhaustion, his clothes haphazard as if he'd grabbed them hurriedly. She moved closer, saying nothing until he looked up and spotted her leaning against the split rail fence.

"Is everything okay?" she asked, sensing that this was not part of the daily routine. She slipped through the fence and began to walk alongside.

He directed a worried look at the horse. "She has colic. If she's not better by dawn, I'm going to have to get the vet out here for her. Last night I thought she was through the worst of it, but Zeke called up at the house about an hour ago and said she was bad again. I just wish to hell I knew what caused it. It's times like these I realize how damned little I know. Chaney says it could be anything, but I feel responsible."

"Is it dangerous?"

"Horses die from it," he said bluntly, his growing concern etched on his harsh features.

With a sense of dismay Marilou looked at the mare, whose coat gleamed silver-gray in the moonlight. "She's so beautiful."

"One of the best. I've got a gorgeous stud picked out for her. If I'm right, her foal could be a stakes winner on the turf. If I can't get her through this, though, it's something I'll never know."

She could feel his frustration along with his compassion. "You don't like not knowing things, do you?"

He shrugged, one hand automatically soothing the mare. "Who does?"

"I'm not talking curiosity. I mean control. That's what's bothering you now. This is a situation you can't control."

He grinned ruefully. "To tell you the truth, I never imagined I'd even be trying to control a situation like this. You should hear Chaney on the subject. He thinks I'm in over my head. Joshua thinks I've gone round the bend. He doesn't comprehend anything that doesn't involve software."

"What about you? What do you think?"

"I think I'd be a damned fool if I didn't admit that Chaney is absolutely right. Right now you couldn't fill the first page of a diary with what I really know about horses. The only reason Chaney gave in and went to bed for a couple of hours was that he knows this morning could be worse and I promised to wake him if she developed a temperature."

"In many ways you seem like an odd pair, but you have a lot of respect for him, don't you?"

"Chaney managed this farm for years before I came along. Some of Florida's top Thoroughbreds were bred here when it was in its heyday. There's not much about horses and breeding he doesn't know. I'm lucky to have him."

"What did you do before?"

He grinned ruefully. "Which year?"

"Can't hold a job, huh?" she teased, knowing instinctively that was far from the truth.

"Can't settle down. I've bought and sold half a dozen businesses in the past twenty years. Making money gets to be a bore."

"I suppose that depends on how easily you do it. I've never had that problem."

"Why'd you pick the post office?"

"I had an 'in.' My Dad had worked there all his life. It's steady work."

"Could you walk away from it?"

"What do you mean?"

"Is it something you care about passionately?"

"Passionately, no. But I like it."

"Then why not leave? Try something you do care about."

The thought of her camera equipment stored in a closet in her Atlanta apartment teased at her. He couldn't know about that, and she wasn't ready to talk about it. Not yet. "Like what?"

"I don't know. Maybe a housekeeping job in Ocala."

Her heart caught, even as she knew deep down that he'd meant the question only hypothetically. She lifted her gaze to meet his and saw him studying her with that same intensity that had so unnerved her the night before. "What are the fringe benefits?" she asked, matching his light, bantering tone.

His lips curved in a faint smile. "A cautious woman. There's a lot to be said for that."

If he'd labeled her lazy or indifferent, she would have been no more irritated. "I didn't set out to be cautious," she said with an edge. "It just happened."

"Hey, why so touchy? There's nothing wrong with caution. Most folks say it's the sensible way to live."

"My parents certainly thought so."

His gaze rested on her consideringly. "Why does that make you so angry?"

"I'm not angry," she snapped. She hadn't realized that her voice had climbed, until the horse nickered nervously and pranced away.

Cal turned his attention to the mare, settling her down, then observed, "You don't seem like a lady who'd be happy all shut up inside. I saw you out on the lawn earlier. You liked the way the grass felt under your feet, didn't you?"

She shrugged, feigning indifference. "That doesn't mean I want to spend my life barefoot."

"You're getting all prickly again, Marilou. I wonder why? Am I hitting too close to home?"

"Maybe so," she conceded grudgingly. "Once, a long time ago, I had other plans."

"What plans?"

"Oh, travel mainly," she said, admitting to only part of the truth. "I wanted to see the world. When I finished college, I was going to take off and explore, try different things."

"Why didn't you?"

"Things didn't work out."

"It's been my experience that you can either make things work out or not. Blaming it on fate or whatever is just an excuse."

She glared up at him, aware that her eyes were filling with tears. "You don't know anything about it, Cal Rivers. You obviously just run from responsibility. I couldn't."

He ignored her charge and asked pointedly, "Responsibility to whom?"

"My parents."

"Were they sick? Did they need your help?"

"They died."

Refusing to look at him, she heard his sharp intake of breath, the low curse, then, "I'm sorry."

His compassion surrounded her and, after all this time of having no one to lean on, made her want to move into his arms and draw on his strength. Instead she said simply, "It's been a couple of years now. I should be over it, but sometimes it sneaks up on me and I realize I'm not."

"Life can deal some pretty lousy blows. There's no set timetable for recovery that I know about. How come you didn't follow through on your plans after they died?"

"Because they had hated the idea. We'd been arguing about it the night of their car accident. It just seemed like the wrong thing to do once they were gone. Disrespectful, somehow. I guess in a way I envy you, being able to walk away without looking back. That's what you do, isn't it? You just take off whenever the mood strikes you?"

"That's about right. Just so you know, though, I never turn my back on my responsibilities. When I sell a business, I make sure my people are taken care of. I owe them that. Most of them wind up better off than they were before I came."

"Do you think security is all you owe them? What about explanations, loyalty?"

"The best loyalty comes in the form of a steady paycheck. That's the beginning and end of what I owe them."

"You can just cut everyone off like that? You certainly vanished from Palm Lane like a man who didn't want anyone following. I had the devil's own time trying to track you down."

"I believe in making clean breaks and starting fresh."

"Breaks are never clean, not unless you make it a point to keep a real distance between you and the people around you. I'm not saying my way's better, but it seems to me that yours is a stupid way to live."

"Maybe so, but I've had a long time to get used to it."

Marilou shuddered and then was filled with a deep sadness. "I'd never get used to it."

"Do you have a man waiting for you back in Atlanta?"

"No, no man," she said to Cal. "Not the way you mean."

"Friends?"

"A few, though a lot of them have left Atlanta the past couple of years."

"Then why go back? Start your adventure now, this minute."

"And do what?"

"Stay here with us. The housekeeping job is yours for as long as you want it. When you're ready to move on, you can."

The idea tempted in a way he'd probably never intended. Not that Cal Rivers wasn't very aware of the impact he'd have on a woman, any woman, but he probably figured he'd warned her adequately about the kind of no-strings man he was.

"How long do you expect to stick around here yourself?" she asked.

"It's hard to say. Right now it's all new. I want to make this stud farm one of the best. That takes time. A few good stallions were part of the original deal, but I want more. In some cases that'll mean buying them as yearlings, training them and giving them time to be tested on the track. I suppose I'd like to have a Kentucky Derby winner just once."

Marilou was surprised by his level of enthusiasm and apparent commitment to such a long-range plan. "Why did you pick this, anyway? It's a far cry from the computer business you had in Daytona."

"You know about that?"

"I discovered it when I was trying to track you down."

"Maybe you've missed your calling. Maybe you ought to be a private eye."

"In some ways I already am. You still haven't answered me. Why a stud farm?"

"It looked like fun," he said with a touch of irony as they took yet another turn around the quarter-mile training track.

"Then you must not have known about these 4:00 a.m. strolls."

"Maybe I just wanted to get into practice for fatherhood."

Marilou swallowed the sudden lump in her throat. "Are you and Lady Mary planning a large family?"

At that the horse pricked up its ears and turned its head toward Marilou. She nickered softly. Cal chuckled. "I think Lady Mary has her own family plans and they don't include me."

Marilou looked from him to the horse and back again. "Lady Mary?"

"Lady Mary," he confirmed.

She felt laughter bubbling up from deep inside, relieved laughter. "Why didn't you tell me last night?"

"It was too much fun watching you jump to conclusions."

Just then Chaney joined them, nodding at Marilou, then looking at the horse. "She doing any better?"

"I think so. She seems to have settled down quite a bit."

"Want me to take over?"

"Let's take her back to the barn and see how it goes," Cal suggested.

"I'll go back and get breakfast on the table," Marilou volunteered.

They both shot her a surprised look. Cal nodded. "We'll be in soon."

As she walked away, she heard Chaney demand, "Is she staying?"

"At least through breakfast, it seems," Cal said. "After that, I guess we'll see."

Marilou couldn't tell from his tone if it mattered to him one way or the other. The apparent indifference set her teeth on edge. She worked out her frustration by cooking the biggest, heartiest breakfast she could think of. By the time Cal and Chaney came back in, she had the food on the table.

"Well, boss, will you look at this," Chaney said with glee, digging into the stack of pancakes she'd kept warm in the oven. Apparently he was willing to overlook his objections about her presence as long as she kept his stomach filled.

Cal grunted. He might be unwilling to acknowledge her new attitude, but she noticed that it didn't keep him from taking five pancakes for himself. "You surprise me," he said, swallowing the last of them. "For a minute there last night, I figured you for one of those types who can't cook a lick."

"Oh, I can cook. I just don't like men making assumptions about the role I should play."

His gaze narrowed. "Sounds like the usual rhetoric to me."

Unintimidated by his fierce look, Marilou scowled right back. He laughed then and shook his head. "Lady, you really are a piece of work. So, tell me, what do you plan to do about clothes? I never met a woman yet who was satisfied to wear the same outfit day after day."

That, of course, was a quandary that had crossed her mind already. She supposed there was no help for it. She was going to have to leave and drive back to her hotel, unless...

"I don't suppose you're ready to discuss this visit to your grandmother yet?"

He pushed back from the table and tilted his chair onto its back legs. Long fingers intertwined and rested on his belt buckle. "Nope."

She sighed. "I was afraid of that."

"You decided about taking me up on my offer?"

"What offer's that?" Chaney asked.

"I thought maybe she'd like to hire on as our housekeeper."

Chaney choked on his coffee, then settled into a sullen pout.

"Hey, you liked the pancakes, didn't you?" Cal teased. "And what about the spaghetti?"

"We wasn't starving before she came."

"The next thing to it. I was ready to start ordering pizza deliveries. What about it, Marilou? You gonna stick around?"

She suddenly realized that she wanted very much to stay, and it had very little to do with the letter anymore. She took a deep breath. "What about a trial run?"

"How long?"

"A month. That's how long my vacation lasts."

He stuck out his hand, enveloping hers. The currents that raced along her arm headed straight for her abdomen, spawning desire and confusion in equal measures. Oh, yes, she thought, she was definitely in over her head, definitely out of her mind.

"I guess I'll go and get my things," she said, lifting her gaze to his. "If you're sure."

"I'm sure." He kept his gaze on her as she cleaned up the kitchen and got her purse.

"I shouldn't be more than a few hours," she said finally, still struggling to determine the wisdom of her decision.

Apparently he read her doubts and misinterpreted them. Frowning, he said, "And here I thought we'd been making progress. I was sure you trusted me to be here when you got back."

"I don't trust you a bit, but I'm going anyway," she said, glad that he couldn't read her so easily. "And don't get your hopes up, because I will be back and I haven't forgotten about the letter, either."

He laughed at that, the first unrestrained emotion she'd seen. "I never doubted that for a minute, sweetheart."

She hesitated at the door, then teased, "Don't change the locks."

"I wouldn't dream of it," he countered with a wink.

If he meant the devilish wink to be a warning of some sort, it failed. Marilou found the challenge of it flat-out irresistible.

Chapter Five

Cal stayed clear of the house until nearly supper time. It was one of the hardest struggles of his life. Oh, he had plenty to do to keep occupied, but all of his thoughts seemed centered on Marilou Stockton. He couldn't imagine a more troubling turn of events. He'd made it a practice not to let any woman get too close. He hadn't lived with a woman for the past ten years, not since he'd realized and accepted that he was the kind of man who simply couldn't settle down and make the kind of commitment any decent woman deserved.

Now he had gone and broken his own rule. He'd invited a woman who was dead set on reforming him to stick around and give it her best shot. Even if he hadn't been convinced of his own lunacy, Chaney would have been more than happy to point it out. His scowling disapproval spoke volumes. As a result of that silent condemnation, Cal flatly refused to be caught looking to see if Marilou had returned, although Chaney was giving him regular reports.

Squinting toward the horizon at midafternoon, Chaney announced obliquely, "Not yet." Obviously he figured that Cal would know perfectly well what he meant.

"Not yet," he said again an hour later and again the hour after that, until Cal felt like strangling him. All of the men were giving him a wide berth as his temper grew shorter with each passing minute.

What if she didn't come back? The prospect nagged at him worse than her presence had. God knew, he couldn't blame her for running scared. There was a contradictory blend of recklessness and caution in her that fascinated him. Maybe the caution had won out. After all, he'd warned her about his life-style in one breath, then with the next he'd taunted her to share it. Even though the invitation to stay had been couched as a job offer, only a totally naive woman would believe that the two of them could keep it that way for long. The air had crackled with sexual tension from the minute they'd laid eyes on each other. He realized with a sudden guilty pang that Marilou might just be too innocent, too hell-bent on proving something to herself to recognize all the snapping and sparring for what it was, a prelude to passion of a different sort entirely. Well, heaven help the two of them if she'd misunderstood!

Cal prided himself on being an analytical man. Some even described him as coolly calculating. He never ever let his emotions get in the way of a business decision. That made this impulsive move all the more disconcerting. There was an emotional tug here that was not only totally out of character, but went against every commonsense instinct he possessed.

Maybe it was her long red hair pulled back in that braid that his fingers itched to undo.

Maybe it was her green eyes, which met his with such a total lack of guile.

More likely—and most dangerous—it was the depth of caring that radiated from her. That compassion had made her travel several hundred miles to find a long-lost grandson for a woman she didn't even know. The part of him that was accustomed to burying family ties wanted to know what sort of woman was driven to do something like that. He wanted that warmth and generosity of spirit directed at him, even as he distrusted it.

It was nearly dusk when he finally spotted the dust flying up on the long driveway to the house. He caught himself grinning as he watched. She drove at a damn-the-consequences speed with which she apparently did everything else regarding him. Relief, so profound it astonished him, flooded through him. Perversely it kept him hiding out down in the stables until long after Chaney had gone to his quarters to clean up for supper.

If Cal had hoped that the defiant gesture would prove his indifference, he was very much mistaken. He had only to walk into the kitchen and see her there to feel the unfamiliar swell of emotion that had plagued him throughout the day.

Marilou was dressed in a flowered sundress that showed off shoulders lightly dusted with freckles and emphasized a tiny waist. He had to fight an almost irresistible urge to circle that waist with his hands and kiss every one of those faint marks left by the sun. As he passed by, he caught the scent of roses, sweet and all too alluring. Strappy little sandals that had no business on a farm showed off her ankles. She had fine ankles, he observed with a catch in his heartbeat. When he saw Chaney regarding them appreciatively, he had to restrain the primitive, proprietary impulse to slug him.

Keeping his purely masculine response under control might have been more difficult if he hadn't been drawn toward the pots simmering on the stove. Chili, thick with meat and beans and spices bubbled in one. In another, ears of sweet corn tumbled in the boiling water. In the last, greens simmered with a ham hock. As he drew in a deep, satisfying breath, he realized that it had been twenty years since he'd had a real home-cooked meal. Hell, maybe longer. His mother hadn't been much of a cook. She'd grown up in a house filled with servants. His daddy's income, once the oil business crashed, hadn't even been enough to support a cleaning woman once a week. After that his mother tended to serve complaints instead of decent meals. The fancy restaurants that had eventually taken the place of frozen dinners as his own career took off were more likely to serve beef Wellington than chili.

"Smells good," he said, recalling the last time he'd eaten real Texas chili. It had been in a diner near the bus station an hour before he'd left home for good. Joshua had been sitting on the stool next to him, talking a mile a minute, coming up with every reason he could think of to keep Cal from running. Not a one of those reasons had been worth a tinker's damn once he'd made up his mind to go. He wondered what Joshua would have to say when he heard about his new, temporary housekeeper.

Marilou turned at the sound of his voice and greeted him with a radiant, unhesitating smile that almost took his breath away. Any sane man would fly home from work for a welcome like that.

"I hope you like chili," she said, a hint of nervousness in her eyes. "I made enough for an army. This kitchen looks as if it were built for the entire crew. I wasn't sure if you'd want some for the other men."

'Not tonight. They're used to going out on their own or cooking out in the bunkhouse. If it looks like you're going to stick around, we'll see if they want to change that."

"They might want to sample my cooking before they make up their minds."

"If that corn bread that's baking tastes half as good as it smells, I can almost guarantee they'll want to join us," he said.

"Amen to that," Chaney agreed, walking in just then and eyeing the big golden squares she was cutting and putting into a basket lined with a bright red-and-white checked napkin. He was reaching for a piece before she could get the corn bread on the table.

"I think you may have found a way to his heart, after all," Cal observed wryly as he sat at the big round table that she'd set with a red-checked cloth and the sturdy white everyday dishes. It occurred to him again that she had an instinct for making things homey instead of fancy. She'd left the previous owner's fine English bone china and expensive Irish crystal in the cupboard where they belonged.

Marilou grinned back at him. "Cooking is a tried and true method. My mother swears she got my father to marry her by baking him mouth-watering lemon meringue pies."

Chaney coughed and shot a warning glance at Cal. "Did you hear that, boss? I guess she's put you on notice. There's a lot to be said for a woman who don't play games."

Marilou blushed prettily at the taunt, but met Chaney's gaze evenly. "Who says it's not you I'm after, you handsome devil?"

Chaney's eyes went wide as half-dollars, and he gobbled down the rest of his meal as if he had to get to a fire. Cal and Marilou both burst into laughter as he muttered his excuses and scrambled away from the table, leaving them to their coconut cake and coffee.

Cal tilted his chair back and watched Marilou grow increasingly nervous. She fussed with her napkin and avoided his gaze as if she'd just realized the new intimacy of their relationship.

"Settle down, girl," he said gently. "I'm not out to ravish you." Yet, he amended silently. He'd never taken a skittish woman yet, and the past few months on the farm had taught him a lot about patience and calming nerves. Unfortunately it had also been a time of celibacy, and a woman as pretty as Marilou could make a man in that condition a little crazy.

"Maybe that's what's bothering me," she said, clearly emboldened by his disclaimer.

His whole body tensed at the unexpected taunt. That flash of daring in her nature was far more dangerous than she realized. "Careful, Marilou. I could change my mind real easy."

She smiled knowingly. "I'm not worried."

"You ought to be, sweetheart. I'm no saint."

"Oh, I know that," she said breezily. "But I also know you're not about to take a chance on involvement, not with a woman who's already underfoot."

"Meaning?"

"That your type of woman probably has one foot on a plane before you dare to kiss her."

The tart observation was so close to the mark, it astounded him. It also worried him a little that she could read him so well, while he couldn't figure her out a bit. She was like a diamond, showing off new facets depending on which way it faced the light. That made her a challenge, and he knew himself well enough to recognize that made her the most dangerous woman he'd met in a long time. Still, instead of keeping his distance, he asked, "What about you? What's kept you single all this time?"

"I'm only twenty-five."

"I'm still surprised some man hasn't snapped you up."

"I'm not running, if that's what you mean. I suppose, if anything, I've just been waiting for the right man to come along."

"What would he be like?"

"Intelligent, adventurous, maybe even a little wild," she said with a grin that reminded him of a teenager sharing secret confidences. "Know anyone who fits those qualifications?"

"What does a woman who bakes corn bread and coconut cake want with a man who's wild?"

"You know what they say, opposites attract."

"Maybe so, but do they last?"

"You're asking the wrong person. I haven't met a man like that yet, much less tried to make the relationship work."

"You could always practice with me," he offered.

He watched as she swallowed hard, then worked to hide her sudden nervousness. "I'm not so sure you're as wild and daring as you'd like me to believe. In fact, I think you might be surprised at just how domesticated you could become if you gave yourself half a chance."

He found himself grinning. "So, based on your analysis, we're not opposites at all?"

"Not deep down."

"Then, according to the theory, there should be no attraction."

"That's right," she said with that devilish gleam reappearing in her eyes.

That glint, like moonlight on emeralds, was yet another challenge he couldn't refuse. He reached out, hooked his hand around a rung of the ladder-back chair and dragged her to him. Before she could recover from the sudden movement, his lips were on hers, catching her soft gasp of surprise. His fingers curved around her bare shoulders, savoring the smooth texture that was like silk against the sandpaper roughness of his calluses. Her hands were pressed against his chest. After one startled push, a faint flutter of protest, they gentled against him. Her tongue, shy and hesitant, touched his lips, then retreated, as if she were afraid to dare more. It was the touch of an angel with the impact of Satan.

No more experienced kiss had ever awakened such wonder, such desperate wanting in him. No sweet touch of innocence had ever stirred such terror. With an anguished moan, he tore himself away and stood up. He couldn't even bring himself to look at her, fearing what he'd see. If there were tears of dismay in her eyes, if he'd frightened her, he'd never forgive himself.

"Go on up to bed," he said gruffly.

"The dishes..."

"Leave 'em. It won't be the first time they sat here overnight."

"You're paying me to do them," she insisted, stacking them by the sink and avoiding his gaze. "And

I have no intention of spending an extra hour in the morning scrubbing off dried food.''

"I'll put them in the damned dishwasher. Now go on, before I do something we'll both regret.''

She sighed then and walked slowly to the door. Only when her back was to him did he risk really looking at her. Her spine was straight and proud. There was no way he could tell how deeply he'd hurt her, until she turned and looked back. To his surprise, there was no condemnation in her eyes, only something that looked faintly like sorrow.

"I think maybe you already have," she told him softly. Then she was gone, leaving the scent of roses trailing behind her and a heavy ache in his heart.

For a man who'd lived his whole life without regrets, Cal realized he'd just filled a whole day with a passel of them.

Cal's kiss had had more force than a tornado sweeping through Georgia. It took three days for Marilou to feel comfortable looking him in the eye again, though she did so with determined regularity. She refused to let him see that he'd shaken her. It was small comfort that he didn't seem to be much easier around her. When he could, he avoided her and left it to Chaney to tell her what time to have meals on the table, where to go for supplies and to write out the checks for household needs.

Marilou was a patient woman, but she was beginning to worry that she was wasting precious time. By now Cal's grandmother could be much worse, and

Marilou hadn't even succeeded in getting him to look at the letter. She'd planned on mentioning it at dinner the night before, but he hadn't come in. Chaney had offered no explanations. He'd just silently eaten his own meal, thanked her in his gruff manner and gone out, leaving Marilou alone with her thoughts and a whole lot of confusing emotions.

It seemed to her that she had two choices. She could wait Cal out, hoping that sooner or later he'd get past this stubbornness on his own. Or she could push him and risk having him toss her and the letter all the way back to Georgia. She finally opted for waiting, at least for a few more days. And since this was supposed to be an adventure, she decided she might as well make the most of it. That night at dinner she asked Chaney if he thought Cal would mind if she did some work in the garden.

"It's a disgrace," she said. "You should see the way the weeds have taken over. You'd have plenty of fresh vegetables if somebody just put in a little effort. I saw some tomatoes and some zucchini. Possibly some green beans. What do you think?"

"Ain't up to me."

"Well, the ground's wasted the way it is. I think I'll just go ahead."

The next day she picked up a half dozen tomato plants, along with seedlings for several other vegetables. She spent an extra half hour getting directions on exactly how to prepare the ground and plant them. She could hardly wait to get started.

As soon as she'd put away the groceries, she put on a pair of shorts and a halter top, then went to the barn for a shovel, a rake and a hoe. Zeke, Roddy and Chaney took one hard look at her and simply stared until she flushed with embarrassment.

"I'll get what you need," Cal growled as he returned to the barn leading Devil's Magic. He handed the horse over to Chaney and shot a stern glance that had Zeke and Roddy scurrying back to work. "If you're going to parade around down here, put some damned clothes on."

She looked down at the shorts and knit top. "For heaven's sakes, people wear less than this at the beach."

"If you were at the beach, you'd fit right in. Around here the only females wearing fewer clothes are the fillies and, believe me, they're not much competition."

She supposed he had a point, though she doubted any of the men in that barn were likely to be stirred to passion by one look at her in this outfit. "Sorry," she apologized anyway. "I didn't think."

His eyes met hers. She noticed he was careful to keep his glance from dropping below her chin. "Next time you will," he said, handing her the gardening equipment. "Don't stay out in that sun too long. It's overcast today. It'll fool you."

She nodded as he vanished. While she worked in the garden she was aware that Cal paused to stare at her every time he returned to the barn, but he never waved or acknowledged her presence in any way. In fact, for all the attention he paid to her, she might have been invisible.

It took her two days to get the garden into shape. The work was far harder than she'd anticipated, but when she was done, when the ground had been turned and watered and the plants were in nice, even rows, she felt a rare sense of accomplishment. There had been something soothing about the task. When it was over, though, she immediately began looking around for something new to try. The Thoroughbreds were the obvious choice.

The next morning, dressed in jeans, a T-shirt and tennis shoes, she presented herself to Chaney. "I want to learn about horses," she announced.

He shoved his hat back on his head and regarded her skeptically. "There's books in the house."

"The horses are here. I figure I'll learn a lot more by doing than I will by reading, don't you?"

"You know anything at all?"

"Nope."

At his disgusted expression, she added, "Just think of me as fresh clay. You get to mold me. I'll do whatever you say."

"I ain't so sure the boss is gonna like this. He hired you to keep house."

"You have any complaints about the food?"

"No."

"When you do, I'll give this up. Come on, Chaney. I really want to learn, and Cal says you're the best."

She could practically see his chest swell with pride. "He's got a point." He stared thoughtfully across the paddock, watching the way Lady Mary was bobbing her head when she caught sight of them. The horse's ears pricked up and she trotted across to them, nuzzling against Chaney's jacket, apparently looking for the sugar cubes Marilou suspected he hid there for all the horses.

Finally, after he'd given Lady Mary the sugar, he turned back to Marilou. "I suppose if you've got your head set on this, you might's well learn things right. I'll start you out at the bottom, though. No favoritism."

"Absolutely. So, what should I do?"

"You can start by mucking out stalls."

"What's that?"

"It ain't anything like baking pies, I can tell you that," he said with a gleeful expression. "Roddy, come on over here and meet Marilou. She wants to learn about horses."

Roddy, who looked to be no more than eighteen or nineteen, gazed at her shyly. He rubbed his hands on his jeans, then held one out to her. "Morning, ma'am," he said in a whisper as she shook his callused hand.

"You let her help you this morning, son. I don't mean watchin', either. Put her to work."

Roddy's cheeks burned and his eyes widened in dismay. "But, Chaney, that ain't no work for a lady."

"No," Marilou said quickly, judging from his reaction that Chaney truly was starting her at the bottom. "It's okay, Roddy. You just show me. I'm not afraid of a little hard work."

He still looked uncertain, but apparently sensed her determination. He nodded at last. "Okay, ma'am. If you say so."

Although she'd begun to figure out just what she'd gotten herself into even before they reached the stable, she was not fully prepared for the overpowering scents that greeted her as Roddy led her into the first stall to be mucked out. He showed her how to rake out the filthy straw and replace it with clean, while the horses were either in the paddock or being worked on the track. Though in many ways the barn was a lot cleaner than she would have imagined, there was no way to keep it spotless. The work was hot, smelly and tiring. The worst of it was that she didn't seem to be learning anything about horses. They weren't even around. She knew better than to complain, though. If Chaney was testing her mettle, she was determined to pass.

By the time he came in to check her work, she had blisters on her hands, straw in her hair and dirt and dust from head to toe.

"She did great," Roddy told the manager. He pointed out the stalls she'd done entirely on her own, and Marilou found herself holding her breath as Chaney inspected them.

"Not bad," he finally said grudgingly.

Marilou felt as if she'd been given a letter of commendation. "Thanks. What about tomorrow?"

He actually came close to smiling at that. "You ain't scared off yet?"

She grinned back at him. "Not a chance."

"Then I'll think on it tonight and we'll figure out a plan."

"Thanks, Chaney."

If nothing else, the hard work had kept her from thinking too hard about Cal. He'd barely crossed her mind all morning. But once she was back at the house, she began to wonder just what he was going to think when he found out what she'd done. Chaney had been right about one thing: Cal was paying her to keep house, not to muck out stalls or even to plant a kitchen garden, for that matter.

She didn't have long to wait. Cal stormed into the kitchen with a scowl she could read from across the room. She immediately turned back to the sink. He came up behind her and reached for one of the blistered hands she was holding under the cool tap water.

At the sight of the raw, broken skin, he muttered an oath. "Sit. Let me get some ointment."

"They'll be fine," she said without moving.

"Not if they get infected," he countered as he reached into a cupboard for a jar of cream. He nudged her toward a chair, then took her hands and soothed on the cool, white ointment. His touch was gentle, but the expression in his eyes was fierce, and Marilou knew he was only holding his anger in check temporarily. The instant he'd treated both hands, those cool gray eyes met hers and there was no doubt about the storm brewing.

"What the devil did you think you were doing?" he demanded roughly. "I kept my mouth shut about the damned garden, but this has gone too far. You're not cut out for this kind of work."

"I won't die from a few blisters."

"Maybe not, but did you ever consider the disruption to my staff? I've got a lovesick groom out there and a manager who's still hooting over the sight of you with straw and horse dung from head to toe."

Marilou did not believe for one minute that Roddy was lovesick or that Chaney had been making fun of her. Cal was making excuses for his own reaction. He didn't like the way she'd wheedled her way into another part of his life.

"I had time on my hands."

"Then clean the damned closets. That's what you're being paid to do."

"The closets are cleaned, and don't forget that this housekeeping game can end just as quickly as it began. You don't take it seriously and neither do I."

"Then why don't you just quit and go home?"

"You know why."

"The letter," he said.

"That's right. The letter. You haven't even asked to see it."

"Fine. What the hell. Show it to me. Then maybe things can get back to normal around here."

"You mean where you're the boss and the rest of us just bow and scrape?"

"No, I mean when I don't have some damned fool woman interfering in my life."

"You read that letter and call your grandmother, and I'll be out of here so fast it'll make your head spin."

"Get the letter," he snapped.

Marilou ran up to her room and retrieved the letter from her purse. Oddly, though, as she took it downstairs, she realized that instead of gloating with satisfaction, what she was feeling felt a whole lot more like pain.

Chapter Six

Cal had no idea why he'd been so infuriated when Chaney had told him about Marilou's working in the barn. All he knew was that the admiring comments from Roddy and the other grooms had made him see red. Then when he'd walked into the kitchen and seen her rinsing her blistered hands at the sink, he'd lost it. Marilou wasn't some fragile little flower needing his protection, but by God he was not going to let her wear herself out while she was working for him.

It wasn't until he was already in the midst of yelling that he had recognized the spark in her eyes for what it was—pride and excitement. She had actually loved spending the day in all that filth. That made him all the madder, because he hadn't been the one to share with her an experience that obviously meant so much.

Talk about perversity! He was getting to be a real genius at it. Now, as payment for his stupidity, he was going to have to read that damned letter.

Read it, hell. If he knew Marilou, that wasn't going to be the end of it. She was going to expect action, and he wasn't ready for a confrontation with his past. The memories had been coming back the past few days, not all of them bad, but enough of them that he wished this so-called grandmother had never tried to track him down.

He was pacing the length of the porch and back again when Marilou returned. Silently she handed him the letter, then retreated to one of the rockers and sat down. The thick vellum paper couldn't have weighed over an ounce or two, but it felt like a ton in his hands. He didn't want to open the envelope, didn't want to know its contents, didn't want to believe that it was really meant for him.

If Marilou had pushed, it would have been easier to rip the letter up right then and there in a gesture of defiance. Or at the very least, he could have blamed her for the way he was feeling. Instead she just rocked and waited, all patience and serenity and expectation.

Finally, itching for a fight, he went over and sat in the chair next to her, still regarding the letter warily.

"What are you afraid of?" she said quietly. "It's just a letter."

"It's the past," he corrected grimly. "And I'm not so sure I want to be reminded of it."

"Why?"

It was something he'd never talked about, not even to Joshua. He figured his friend had seen enough and guessed the rest. Even if that hadn't been the case, Cal wasn't the kind of man who liked baring his soul. A man dealt with his problems; he didn't share them. He stiffened instinctively at Marilou's question, but then he looked into her eyes and there was that tenderness again, that genuine caring. He sighed and, to his amazement, the words just began to come.

Keeping his gaze riveted on the horizon, he said slowly, "From the day I was born about the only thing I can remember about my parents is the fights. Nothing was ever good enough for my mother. Nothing. My father tried and tried, but no matter what he said or did, she was always looking for more." He turned to her. "Do you see? A man can be destroyed by that kind of selfishness and greed."

"Was your father destroyed by it?"

He shrugged. "No," he admitted, still bemused by that. "For some reason he never seemed to blame her. It was like he believed she had a right to be angry and hateful."

"Did they ever explain?"

"I never asked. I just got out as soon as I could and swore I'd never let any woman do to me what my mother did to my father."

"But maybe she had her reasons. Don't you at least want to understand what they were?"

"There's nothing that could make what she did right. Maybe things didn't turn out exactly the way she'd expected, but she had no call to treat him the way she did."

"I'm not trying to make excuses for her. I just think maybe the letter will help you to understand. She may have felt very much alone."

The certainty in her tone made him ask, "Did you read it?"

She nodded, her expression at once full of guilt and apology. "I wasn't supposed to, except to look for an address, but then I saw that your grandmother was dying and I had to read it all. I could see how important it was to her to try to find you. Read it, Cal. Maybe it'll make up a little for what you lost."

He tried once more to convince her—and himself—that he was beyond the reach of the past. "I didn't lose so much, just a harridan of a mother and a spineless father. I gained a lot more: success, satisfaction, power."

She regarded him doubtfully, obviously unimpressed by his accomplishments. "I suppose that is a lot by some standards, but in my book it doesn't make up for family. Seems to me all the money in the world can't compensate for loneliness."

"Don't kid yourself, Marilou. I am rarely lonely."

"Maybe," she said, but he could tell she wasn't buying it. Still the truth of the matter was, he'd never known what loneliness meant until he'd forced himself to spend the past few days staying clear of her. Even now he was drawn to her in a way that warned him to run, to flee the hurt that always, always came with caring.

And yet he stayed, weighing the letter in his hand, trying not to see the expectancy in her eyes as she waited. Finally, with a sigh of resignation, he opened the envelope and withdrew the pages with their crimped scrawl.

My dearest Cal...
I know you'll be surprised to hear from me after all these years. For all I know you didn't even know I existed. I can't really blame your mother for that. It was my fault for being so pigheaded. If you inherited anything from our side of the family, I hope it wasn't that. Stubbornness can be a blessing and a curse. In my case, it cost me everything I held dear, and I believe if your mother is at all honest with herself, she'd have to say the same.

You see, I thought your mother was making a dreadful mistake when she married your father. I had nothing against him, though she was too young and rebellious to realize that. I just knew that I'd spoiled her. She'd been raised to expect so much, things I suspected your father would never be able to provide. Asking a man to give what's beyond him is a terrible thing. No marriage can survive it. I ought to know. I did the same thing to your grandfather and he left me. I could see all the same problems coming with Sissy and your father and it broke my heart.

Still, I should never have caused a rift so deep it could last a lifetime. And once done, I should have had the will to fix it, but I kept waiting for her to come back. I guess she couldn't bear to admit I was right, and I know I was. The people I hired to keep an eye on her whereabouts told me that much. Later, when you were born, I wanted so much to mend fences, but when I wrote, she ignored my letters. I guess after waiting so long, I can't really blame her.

Never forget that I love you, boy. I'm so sorry that we've never had a chance to get to know each other. I'm dying now, so I don't know if we'll ever meet. Just know that not a day goes by when I don't think of you with all my love. Be happy, Cal, and forgive an old woman for her mistakes.

Your grandmother.

Cal's eyes were blurred with tears as he came to the end. He'd never thought of himself as sentimental, but he found that his heart was filled with anguish over all the pain his grandmother must have suffered for that one strong-willed mistake. He knew all about digging in his heels and then learning to live with the consequences. She'd been right, but as she said, at what cost? So much bitterness. So many years of loneliness and regrets. To his surprise he found he was incapable of placing blame, not with her anyway. At last he had a few of the answers to questions that had always plagued him. The relief this brought him was not nearly as complete as he'd hoped. Anger didn't fade that quickly, and nothing she'd said absolved his parents.

He lifted his head and saw that Marilou was studying him closely.

"You believe me now, don't you?" she said softly. "You know she's your grandmother."

"I can't deny that it all fits," he admitted reluctantly.

"Then you'll go see her?"

Not really surprised by the question, he shook his head. "No. There's no need."

"Cal, she's dying. She needs to see you."

"Seeing me won't relieve her guilty conscience. The only one who could do that is my mother, and I doubt she'd feel so inclined."

"You could call her. She should know about this, too."

He stared at her incredulously. "You've got to be kidding. I haven't seen or spoken to my mother for twenty years, not since the day I walked out."

"Then it's about time you did."

"You read the letter. My grandmother knows where to find my mother. It's between the two of them."

"And you can just leave it at that?" she said furiously. "What kind of man are you? Do you have so many people in your life that you can afford to throw away a woman who loves you as much as she obviously does?"

"Grow up, Marilou," he said fiercely, then muttered a curse as he saw her wince. He softened his tone, but not his message. "This isn't some romantic story with a guaranteed happy ending. Pieces of paper and pretty sentiments don't make up for years of anger.''

"They aren't just pretty sentiments. She means it, Cal. She's sorry. You have to go. You have to let her die in peace. If you don't, especially now that you know, the guilt will eat away at you for the rest of your life.''

"What do you know about guilt, my little innocent?'' He couldn't hide the edge of sarcasm that crept into his thoughts. He was tired as hell of her pious attitude about what was right for him.

Her rocking chair stilled and she stared up at him, her expression bleak except for the furious sparks in her eyes.

"You think I don't know anything about guilt?'' she began quietly. "Believe me, Cal Rivers, you don't hold an exclusive on it. I've been living with it since the day my parents died in that accident. I've blamed myself for every bitter word. I've lain awake nights wondering whether they might have avoided the crash if they hadn't been so upset and worried about our argument.''

Huge tears were welling up in her eyes, shimmering on her lashes. For the second time in minutes, Cal felt his own eyes grow misty with the unfamiliar sting of salt. Sorrow and guilt over his harsh accusation lay heavily in his chest as her voice fell to a broken whisper. "I never had the chance to tell them I was sorry. I never told them how much I loved them. Now I'll never get to say the words or to hug them or even to say good—''

With the break in her voice came tears, spilling down her cheeks as she gazed at him helplessly. "Oh, Cal, I miss them so much."

Without thought for the consequences, he lifted her up and gathered her close, sheltering her in his embrace. If he was inexperienced at being comforted, he was even more so at offering it. He murmured nonsense at first, then searched for more, for words that could ease her pain. "I know, babe. I know," he soothed. "They knew how much you loved them, even if you never said the words."

"How?" she asked, clinging to him, watching him with so much hope in her eyes, needing forgiveness he had no right to give. "You can never assume that people know what's in your heart."

"With you, it's possible," he promised. "You're the kind of woman who radiates love. Anyone who knows you would have to feel it. Your parents would be proud of you, Marilou. They taught you to love and to fight for what you believe in. Even though you argued on that last day, I'll bet they were proud to see you standing up for what you wanted in life. Hell, even though your nagging drives me crazy sometimes, I have to admire your conviction. It's who you are."

She wiped away her tears with the back of her hand, the gesture reminding him of a child trying to salvage pride after an outburst. A sad smile tugged at her lips. "Then I guess you won't mind that I'm not going to let up about this. I may not be able to convince you today, but I will sooner or later."

He laughed ruefully. "You are almost as stubborn as I am."

"Let that be a warning to you. I never give up. In my job that's a requirement."

Something about her words stung his pride. He broke free and took a step away, distancing himself from the inexplicable hurt. "So that's why you've been hanging around? You just can't walk away until you've done your job?"

Obviously she heard the tension and irritation in his tone. She frowned as she met his gaze, then looked even more unsettled. She poked her hands in her pockets and glanced down at the ground.

"What else could it be?" she asked in a voice barely above a whisper. That shy question lured like the rustle of satin sheets.

"Maybe this," he said, dragging her back into his arms. He fastened his gaze on hers and murmured again, "Maybe this."

When his mouth claimed hers, the kiss was fueled by anger. He was deliberately rough, taking possession in a way that left no room for doubts about his intentions. It was time she recognized what was happening between them. This was between grown-ups now, the wild flaring of desire as hot and intense as any he had ever known. If he'd thought about it, he would have labeled it branding, but he was beyond thought. His body was hard and aching and needy. Marilou was soft and sweet and every bit as needy. She met spark with flame and made no apologies for it. Perhaps if she had, if she'd shown only the tiniest hint of reservation, he would have been able to stop with that one deep, drugging, mistaken kiss.

Instead, with her willing in his arms, he wanted more. He wanted to taste the sweet skin at the nape of her neck, to feel the weight of her breasts against his palm, to touch and excite and possess. Her whimpers of pleasure, the flaring of excitement in her green eyes, the way she fit herself against the hard contours of his body, all were the gestures of a woman who wanted claiming, a woman who felt the same passion, the same need that he did. The emotions that rioted deep within him suddenly made him angry and as scared as he'd ever been in his life. He wouldn't let this woman touch him, wouldn't allow her to reach the places in his soul that were still raw from past hurts.

He smoothed away the wisps of hair that framed her face, studying the lush lips that were still parted and moist from his kisses. He rubbed the pad of his thumb over the silk of her cheek, then across a bottom lip that quivered at his touch. It all felt so good, so right, which made it vital that he prove to himself and to her how wrong it was.

"This is why you stayed, isn't it?" he whispered, moving his hands over her, shaping the curve of her hip, cupping her bottom until she was tight against him. The look in his eyes and his words were deliberately provocative, just one phrase shy of crude. He'd show her where things stood, then watch her run. With his touch bold and his voice low and thick with innuendo, he murmured, "When it comes right down to it, this is what it's all about between a man and a woman. You want me as much as I want you."

She met his gaze then with a look that began as longing, then quickly turned to reproach as his meaning settled in. If he'd forced her upstairs and into his bed, she could have looked no more injured. He waited for satisfaction to come. Instead regret slammed into him, and he backed away as if he'd been burned and she were the flame.

"Damn," he muttered, suddenly confused and blaming her for it. "You're better at making a man feel guilty with one look than somebody else could with a whole dictionary full of words."

She reached up and touched his face. "I'm not trying to make you feel guilty. At least not about this. You're right. I do want you every bit as much as you want me. I'm not liar enough to even try to deny what's plain as day to both of us. But not like this, Cal. Not when the motivations are all tangled up."

"Hell, honey, when it comes to sex, motivations pretty much stay tangled."

"Then I guess that's something we'll just have to work on along with all the rest."

Amazed by her calm acceptance of what had very nearly happened between them and the way he'd tried to make it into something primitive and sordid rather than beautiful, he regarded her warily. "You're not going to run like a scared rabbit?"

She grinned at him then, a wobbly smile that was sheer bravado. His heart lurched unsteadily. She was so beautiful, so incredibly desirable and so damned gullible and innocent. She was no match for a man who'd always had few scruples when it came to women.

"So," she teased, "that's what you were hoping. It's going to take more than an offer of your manly charms to scare me off, Cal Rivers, so you might as well get used to having me around."

He shook his head in genuine bewilderment. "It occurs to me that you actually enjoy testing a man's patience," he said, delighted laughter suddenly threading through his voice.

"I'm beginning to think maybe I do," she admitted. "And you're such an easy subject."

"Careful, sweetheart. I'm dangerous when I'm provoked."

"So you keep warning me. But like I said, I don't scare easy."

His whole body pulsing with awareness and frustration, Cal conceded the round. "Maybe I do," he muttered, leaving before the temptation to kiss her again grew overwhelming.

Several hours and several drinks later he was on the phone to Joshua, the one person in the world who knew just about everything there was to know about him.

"Cal, do you know what time it is?" his friend grumbled sleepily.

"Sometime after one, I suppose," Cal said unapologetically. "I haven't checked the clock since midnight."

"Hasn't anyone ever explained the concept of business hours to you?"

"On occasion. I'm not calling to discuss business."

That seemed to wake Joshua right up. "Oh?"

"What do you know about Marilou Stockton?"

"Who?"

"Don't play games. I know she called you."

"Oh, wait," he said thoughtfully. "I remember now. She was looking for you a couple of weeks back. Are you telling me she found you?"

"She found me all right. You must have sent her straight to me."

"I didn't tell her a damn thing. You know me better than that. What's she after? She's not some woman you ran out on, is she? Her name didn't sound familiar."

Cal caught himself grinning ruefully. "Where did you ever get the idea that I've told you about every woman in my life?"

"Good Lord! You mean there are more?"

"Very funny."

"Cal, as fascinating as this conversation is, I have a 7:00 a.m. breakfast meeting. Could we cut to the chase?"

"She's here."

"Now? At one in the morning?"

"She's been here."

"Since when?"

"Since two weeks ago."

Joshua, damn him, chuckled. "Well, well. How did that come about?"

"I hired her," he admitted miserably. "Stop laughing, dammit."

"Sorry. I can't help it. Maybe you'd better explain. Exactly what did you hire her to do? I didn't have the impression she was even looking for a job."

"She wasn't. It was just temporarily, as a housekeeper. At least that's the way it started, but now I'm not sure how to go about getting rid of her."

"Why do you want to? Is she stealing the silver?" Joshua inquired, too cheerfully, it seemed to Cal.

"No," he said, aware that a bleak note had crept into his voice. "Why doesn't matter. I just think she ought to go."

"Then fire her. You used to be pretty good at that, as I recall."

"I only fired you once, and even then I couldn't make it stick. I think you'd better take care of this for me."

"Me? Since when did I ever get involved in your personnel problems?"

"Since I just made it part of your job description."

"Is there something more here that I should know about?"

"Nothing," Cal denied emphatically.

"Which means there's something. Why don't you drive over tomorrow and we can talk about it?"

"I'm leaving town in the morning. Take care of this before I get back," he said, and hung up before Joshua could argue with him. The phone rang within seconds. It rang again five minutes later. When it started ringing again ten minutes after that, he picked it up reluctantly.

"No," Joshua said in response to his growled greeting. "But I think maybe I will drive out to see what this is all about. She must really be something if she's got you running scared."

"I am not running scared," he said emphatically, something the last two shots of Scotch made difficult to pull off.

"And I'm Secretariat," Joshua said, chuckling again. "You sure lead an interesting life, old friend. Just watching you keeps me young."

"Oh, go to hell," Cal grumbled, figuring that was where he was going to end up after tonight anyway. He might as well have company.

Chapter Seven

Marilou wasn't all that surprised by Cal's disappearance after that searing kiss and their conversation about the desire that was growing between them. Running seemed to be his way of dealing with unwanted emotions. She knew that and yet, with her whole body still aching with longing, she'd listened until well after midnight for the reassuring sound of his footsteps on the porch. If he'd come in, though, it had been after she'd fallen asleep.

Now, edgy with anticipation, she was putting dishes on the table for breakfast and fixing the ham, eggs and cheese grits she'd discovered were his favorite breakfast. Chaney came in, nodded, then stuck a napkin in the open throat of his blue chambray work shirt and silently began to eat. Marilou sat down across from him and began picking at her breakfast, her gaze going constantly to the screen door.

"He's gone," Chaney said finally in a flat tone that told her he wasn't too happy about it.

Startled, she stared at him. "Gone? You mean he's out with the horses already?"

"I mean gone. Took the trailer and a couple of the men and headed up to Kentucky. Dang fool thing, if you ask me. Should have flown and saved all that time. The men could have taken the trailer up. Tried to tell him that, but no, he was dead set on getting out of here this morning. Left here at five." He regarded her knowingly. "Any idea why he was in such a blamed hurry?"

She swallowed hard, sensing the undercurrent of disapproval in Chaney's tone. "He didn't say anything to me," she responded defensively. "Why did he go? He must have said."

"Said he wanted to get up there early for the spring horse sales. He's hoping to pick up a couple of good yearlings."

Though she hadn't known when the sales were scheduled, she knew how important they were. Cal and Chaney had been discussing them practically since the day she'd arrived. "You let him go alone for that?"

Chaney hooted at that. "I don't *let* the boss do nothing. He does what he dang well pleases. You might do well to remember that yourself, missy. Can't hog-tie a man that's spent his whole life independent."

She glared at him, filled with indignation at Chaney's interpretation of events since her arrival. "I have no desire to hog-tie anyone, and you know perfectly well what I meant. You both agree that you know more about horses than he does. Why didn't you go? Was it because he left earlier than you'd planned?"

Chaney shrugged. "I wasn't planning to go in the first place. I studied the catalogue with him. We talked about which horses he should take a look at. He's got to get his feet wet some time. Man like him operates best when he makes his own mistakes. That's one way to learn real fast."

"But what can you tell from a picture? Don't you have to look at the horse? What if it can't move?"

"I've been teaching him all about conformation. They have photographers trained to shoot the horse just to show off the way he's made. The boss'll recognize good conformation when he sees it. And if the danged horse can't move, don't you think he'll notice? The man may be a greenhorn, but he ain't blind."

"I suppose," she said as she settled into a funk.

Her month's vacation was nearly half over. Even after yesterday's apparent breakthrough, she still hadn't gotten Cal to agree to an actual visit with his grandmother. How was she supposed to work on convincing him when he was hundreds of miles away for who knows how long? How was she supposed to decide about going or staying herself without him around to let her know what he was really thinking? What did she even want with a man who could dismiss family ties so easily? He'd probably forget her just as readily, locking her away in the past with all the other memories he considered too painful to deal with.

In fact, if she were to go by yesterday alone, he'd probably say goodbye and good riddance. He'd be pleased to be rid of her nagging. Even so, he might not be quite so pleased to be robbed of her kisses, no matter how hard he'd worked to make them into something ugly and demeaning. She wasn't so naive that she couldn't recognize wanting when it was pressed square against her. A tiny sigh of longing escaped before she could restrain it.

Chaney regarded her with something that almost looked like sympathy. He muttered his thanks for breakfast, then headed for the door. Twisting his hat in his hand, he stood in the doorway. "In case you was wondering, it'd be my guess that he'll be back by Monday."

"I wasn't wondering," she lied.

"Well, like I said, just in case." He hesitated, still fiddling uncomfortably with his hat.

"Is there something else?"

"I don't suppose you'd want to help out again today."

"I'm probably just in the way," she said morosely.

If she'd hoped for a denial, she'd picked the wrong man. There wasn't a diplomatic bone in Chaney's body, no matter how much pity he was feeling toward her. "Let's face it," he pointed out. "You still got a lot to learn."

"I know that."

"Even so, your help would still be welcome while Zeke and Pedro are on the road with Cal."

Her mood brightened a little. "You mean it?"

"Hell, gal, I don't say things I don't mean. You should know that much by now. See Roddy when you're ready. He'll tell you what to do."

"Thanks, Chaney. I'll be there as soon as I get these dishes scrubbed up."

He nodded curtly, slid his hat on his head and left. His gruff invitation pleased her as nothing else could have. She knew better than to believe that she was more help than hindrance, but the fact that he'd asked at all told her volumes about the fact that he was beginning to accept her.

As soon as she'd straightened up the kitchen and run the vacuum, she put on her work jeans and a long-sleeved shirt, tying the shirttail in a knot at her waist. Anticipating the next few hours of hot, sweaty work with surprising enthusiasm, she started toward the stables, then paused at the sight of dust swirling on the long, winding driveway. Her pulse kicked into high speed.

Maybe it was Cal coming back, she thought as she walked back toward the house. But when the car rounded the final curve in the driveway, she saw that it was an unfamiliar Lincoln, long and black and impressive despite its layer of fresh dust.

The man who stepped out was equally impressive with his broad shoulders, impeccable navy-blue suit, Italian loafers and a face that had been lovingly chiseled into angles similar to Cal's. The perfection might have been too much were it not for the slight bend in his nose, indicating that at one time at least this man had played hard and gotten his nose bloodied in the process. Right now there was curiosity written all over that handsome face, so much so that it had Marilou blushing as she went to greet him. Even before he introduced himself, she guessed that this was Priscilla's hunk, Joshua Ames. Cal could not possibly know two men of calendar caliber.

"You must be Marilou Stockton," he said, holding out his hand.

"How did you know?"

"Cal mentioned you were here. I must say I was impressed with your resourcefulness in tracking him down."

"Were you?" she said doubtfully. "He probably gave you hell for it."

"Actually, he did, but I swore I didn't give anything away."

She grinned. "Oh, but you did. Not much, mind you, but enough for me to figure out the rest."

"But all I said was . . ." His voice trailed off in genuine bewilderment. "I didn't say anything. I know I didn't."

"You admitted he was still in Florida."

He blinked and rubbed a hand across his eyes. "I must be spending too much time at my computer. How did you get from that piece of information to a farm in Ocala?"

"That's my secret, Mr. Ames."

"Call me Joshua. All my friends do."

"And are we going to be friends?" she inquired bluntly.

His blue eyes searched her face for several impossibly long minutes before he nodded. "Yes, I think we are. Where's Cal?"

"On his way to Kentucky."

His face registered astonishment, which rapidly gave way to amusement. "Well, well, the coward ran after all."

Something about his comment told Marilou that Joshua had a pretty good idea of what had gone on between the two of them. "I'm surprised you didn't know about the trip," she said with feigned innocence. "When did you speak to him last?"

"About one o'clock this morning," he said, confirming her suspicions.

"Well, well," she said, mimicking him.

He caught the amusement in her eyes, and suddenly the two of them were laughing. "I'm sorry you wasted a trip," she said finally.

"Believe me, I don't consider it a waste, though why anyone would want to live out here is beyond me, especially a man like Cal."

"Meaning?"

"He's a city boy with an incredible head for business. He belongs in boardrooms, not out here mowing grass."

"I don't think he mows much grass, actually. He spends most of his time with the horses or studying up on breeding. Believe me, he takes this seriously as a business. Come with me, I'll show you around. There are some gorgeous horses in his stables already."

Joshua actually shuddered. "No, thank you. If you have a glass of iced tea, I'd be grateful for it. Then I'll be on my way back into town. I think I've seen enough."

"Meaning me," she said, amusement in her voice. "Did I live up to your expectations?"

"I had no expectations," he contradicted. It was a halfhearted denial. He didn't seem to feel especially guilty about being so obvious. When Marilou regarded him skeptically, he admitted, "Okay, I was a little worried you might be some sort of gold digger. It wouldn't be the first time some woman has gone after Cal for his money."

"I don't want his money, Joshua. I don't even want him. I just want to see him reunited with his family."

Shock registered on Joshua's face. "Good Lord! Does he know that?"

"Oh, he knows it." Her gaze narrowed. "Have you known Cal a long time?"

"Most of his life."

"What can you tell me about his relationship with his family?"

"You'll have to ask Cal. I don't gossip about my clients or my friends. Cal is both."

She nodded. "He made a good choice, then, in trusting you."

"I will say one thing, though. I wish you luck. It's past time for him to be making peace with his past."

Joshua quickly changed the subject then, asking Marilou personal questions about her own background in a way that told her anyone dealing with Joshua Ames would always have to be on their toes. As they finished their iced tea, she realized that she'd given away far more than she'd learned during the brief visit. Still, she had genuinely liked and trusted him.

Walking him back to his car, she said sincerely, "I'm glad we had a chance to meet, but I am sorry you didn't get to see Cal."

"Forget it. You're much prettier than he is," he said.

"Will you come to dinner when Cal gets back?" she asked.

"I'm not so sure I can stand this much fresh air again. Get Cal to bring you over to Daytona."

She grinned at him. "Is this your way of telling me you've decided he's safe out here with me?"

"I guess that's one way of looking at it. Mind if I give you one piece of advice?" he asked, his expression suddenly sober.

"Of course not."

"I still don't know exactly what business about his family brought you here, but Cal is a man who's had his heart broken one too many times. I think whatever your reason for coming, he's far more attracted to you than he's admitted even to me. If he doesn't mean anything to you, you might want to think about going before he gets back."

Marilou nodded.

He touched her cheek. "No offense?"

"No. I'm glad you care enough about him to speak your mind. I'll be honest with you. I don't know how things will end up between the two of us, but I care enough to stick around and find out." She sighed ruefully. "Judging from today's escape, I'm not so sure Cal is equally open to the possibilities."

"He'll come around once he sees that you're not playing games with him. Just be sure that's what you want."

"I'll think it through. I promise."

"Then that's good enough for me."

Over the next few days, Joshua's advice was constantly on her mind. She reveled in the back-breaking work that Chaney assigned, because it made it easier to get through the lonely nights when her thoughts strayed invariably to Cal and the relationship that was blossoming so unexpectedly between them, a relationship fraught with complications. Despite the difficulties, she'd felt a greater sense of fulfillment here than she had in all the months she'd worked for the post office.

The work got easier day by day. She was a quick learner, Roddy told her, blushing. Chaney nodded his agreement. When she asked, he told her which of the books in Cal's office she ought to read first, and that was how she spent the evenings. She curled up in Cal's big leather chair, which still carried the lingering scent of him, and read about the world of Thoroughbreds and the science—or mere theory, according to some—of breeding the best.

More nights than not that's where she fell asleep, the books and magazines tumbling from her lap as she shifted to find a comfortable position. That's where she was when Roddy pounded on the door, shouting her name at three in the morning. She scrambled from the chair and ran.

"Roddy, what is it?"

"It's Winning Pride. She's about to have her foal. You said you wanted to watch. Chaney sent me to get you."

Excitement raced through her. Pulling on Cal's denim jacket as she ran, they reached the barn just in time to see the beautiful mare drop a foal the exact same ebony as its sire, Devil's Magic. From its mother, it had inherited a white blaze on its head.

"We've got us a beauty, a little filly," Chaney announced.

A deep sense of awe filled Marilou as the mother cleaned up the foal, then moved away. Finally on legs that seemed skinny as matchsticks and twice as wobbly, the foal struggled to stand upright. Winning Pride nickered softly and her offspring took one tentative step and then another until she was close enough to tuck her head and suckle as her mother stood patiently. Marilou longed for her camera, wishing once again that she hadn't been so determined to leave photography locked away in the past. Maybe someday Cal would let her come back during foaling season to take pictures of the miraculous moments.

Roddy went to work cleaning up after the birth, and Chaney ran his hands swiftly and knowingly over the newborn, finally pronouncing her fit. The whole thing had taken no more than an hour.

"You going back up to the house?" Chaney asked.

Marilou shook her head, her gaze still fastened on the mare and filly as if she could memorize the image as indelibly as she could have captured it on film. "I want to stay awhile longer."

"Can't say as I blame you," he admitted. "It's an awesome thing to see the first time."

"Can you tell if she'll be a runner?"

"Some say you can. I always like to see 'em on a track before I make a prediction like that." He grinned. "Then again, ain't no sure thing even then."

"Does she have a name yet?"

"The boss had a couple in mind, but he'll have to register them with the Jockey Club and make sure they're okay. I suppose he'll be wanting to do that before he settles on one."

"Do you know what they were?"

"Can't say as I recall."

"Then I'm going to call her Dawn's Magic."

"That's a right pretty name. Fits her, too."

Marilou grinned. "Think I can make it stick?"

"I ain't a betting man anymore, but I'd guess you could get just about anything you wanted out of the boss."

Marilou looked at him in amazement. "Why would you think that?"

"You're still here, ain't you," he said, chuckling as he walked off and left her to think about what he'd said.

Chilled by the cool night air, she found a blanket and wrapped it around her shoulders, then settled into a corner to watch Winning Pride and her foal. That bonding, as natural an instinct as breathing, was something she longed to experience. She wasn't so old yet that she felt the ticking of her biological clock, but age didn't seem to have much to do with the desire to become a mother. Maybe it was just that she'd spent these past few months so absorbed with the idea of family. She fell asleep wondering idly—and dangerously—what a child of hers and Cal's would be like. Stubborn and willful were the two characteristics that came to mind.

The sight that greeted Cal when he stepped into the barn almost took his breath away. Pale golden rays of sun slanted through the windows and turned Marilou's hair into a radiant halo. The loose strands were tangled with the straw of her impromptu bed. Her lips were curved into the beginning of a smile, suggesting pleasant dreams or the faint memory of whatever had been on her mind when she fell asleep. She was wearing his denim jacket, which was several sizes too big for her. It had fallen open, and the thin cotton of her blouse was stretched taut across her breasts. Princess, the fat marmalade cat, had deserted Devil's Magic and was curled against Marilou's side. He hoped the desertion wasn't permanent. Otherwise, he'd have one nasty stallion on his hands.

He stood perfectly still, afraid of waking her, afraid of going any closer. He'd lived the past few days in a torment of desire and doubts. Getting close to her while those thoughts still raged, and with her looking so damned vulnerable and seductive, was courting disaster.

He sighed and took a reluctant step back, but not in time. Winning Pride sensed his presence and whinnied softly, as if to draw his attention to the new filly Chaney had told him about the minute he'd pulled into the yard. Unable to walk away, he crept closer and whispered, "She's a beauty, all right." Even as the words crossed his lips, he knew they could be applied equally to the foal and to Marilou, who shifted restlessly on her bed of straw. Princess meowed indignantly at being disturbed.

Suddenly Marilou's eyes blinked wide and she scrambled into a sitting position, dragging her fingers through the tangles of her hair. "Cal, you're back."

"Miss me?" he said lightly, not really expecting her to admit to it, not even willing to admit how much he wanted her to.

She nodded sleepily, too groggy to hide her instinctive reaction. His breath caught at the innocent admission. His gaze fastened on hers and he felt the familiar heat rising, that first soft stir of yearning. He'd been so sure that a few days of distance would calm his frayed nerves, would plant all the warnings clearly in his brain. Instead his blood ran every bit as hot and wild as it had before he left.

"There are more comfortable beds in the house," he noted, then regretted even the reference to a bed when she was all sleep-tousled and desirable.

"But none this close to the action."

He found himself grinning at her excitement. "There's something to be said for being a farm girl, isn't there?"

"If you'd told me a few weeks ago that I'd be helping out at the birth of a foal, I'd have sworn you were crazy. The idea would have scared me to death, but the reality, my God, Cal, it's like nothing I've ever experienced before. Not that I did all that much. Winning Pride did all of the work. Still, I don't think I'll ever forget it."

"Chaney says you have a name all picked out."

She blushed. "I know I don't have the right. You have a name all ready for submission, but I couldn't help it."

"What's your choice?"

"Dawn's Magic, for when she was born, for her sire and for what she meant to me."

Winning Pride pricked up her ears and bobbed her head. Cal laughed. "Seems like the mama approves."

Marilou grinned. "Is it up to her?"

"Seems like her right. I'll pass it by the Jockey Club and see if anyone else has a claim on it."

"Thank you." She held his gaze for far too long, long enough to make his heart thunder and his thoughts rove again into dangerous territory. As if she sensed the shift in mood, she blinked and said hurriedly, "My heavens, Cal, you must be starved. Why didn't you say something? I'll go up right now and fix breakfast."

"There's no need to hurry. I want to see the new horses settled before I come up."

"The trip was successful?"

"I thought so," he said, then grinned ruefully. "We'll see what Chaney has to say when he sees what I've brought home."

She laughed. "There's something to be said for a man who values honesty above tact."

"It can be a little rough on the ego, though."

"I can certainly vouch for that."

"He says you've been doing a good job."

"He likes my blueberry muffins."

"I mean with the horses."

Her eyes widened with pleasant surprise. "He said that?"

"And more," he teased. "But I think I'll keep the rest to myself."

She blushed and started back to the house.

"Marilou."

"Yes?"

"I'm glad you stayed."

"I hired on for a month. I didn't want to go back on my word."

"I would have understood if you had," he said. Left unsaid was how terrified he'd been that she would go, scared off by his nasty temper and blatant advances.

He'd realized while he was gone that he wasn't going to shake off his feelings for her quite as easily as he'd hoped. That figured out, he had only to decide how best to understand them. The only way to do that, it seemed to him, was to get this issue of that damned letter settled once and for all. With that out of the way, maybe then they could figure out what there really was between them. Maybe they'd discover that the letter was the only glue holding them together at all. It was what a part of him hoped ... and what the rest of him somehow dreaded.

It was nearly an hour before he finally made his way back to the house. Chaney came out just as he reached the back door.

"I put the horses in the barn by the new paddock," Cal told him. "As soon as I eat, I'll be back down to see what you think of them. You were right about that Seattle Slew colt. The price went too high. It just about killed me to do it, but I finally backed out of the bidding."

"Ain't no sense going into hock for an untried horse. There's plenty of potential with some of the others if you know what to look for. You're gonna have to start looking for a trainer now. Whether you want to hire one here or send the horses out, it's time."

"My inclination is to hire our own. Think about it, Chaney. See if any names come to mind. When I come back out, we'll talk about it. I don't want to do anything on this without your say-so."

Chaney nodded. "I've got some ideas. A lot depends on how much you're willing to spend."

"I told you when we started up that I would spend what it took to make this place the best. That hasn't changed."

"Glad to hear it."

Cal studied his manager closely, convinced that there was something on the old man's mind. "You got something else to say?"

"Nothing that can't wait until you've had your breakfast."

"Come on. You might's well spit it out before you choke on it."

A frown creased Chaney's brow and his eyes grew serious. "What're you gonna do about her?"

"Marilou?"

Chaney looked disgusted at his deliberate obtuseness. "You know any other females around here?"

"Okay. What do you want me to say?"

"Is she going or staying?"

"That's up to her."

"You ain't got no opinion on the matter?"

"None I care to discuss."

"I ain't asking you to discuss 'em with me, so long as you discuss 'em with her. Seems to me she's got a right to know where she stands around here."

Cal nodded. "I'll keep that in mind."

Chaney's expression turned even more sour. *"I'll keep that in mind,"* he mimicked under his breath. Glaring at Cal, he added, "If you ask me, that ain't no way to treat a lady. Not that you asked me, of course."

Cal grinned at the unexpected championing of Marilou. "You must really like her blueberry muffins."

"I don't know what they've got to do with anything." He threw up his hands. "You just go on and do whatever you dang well please. Suppose you will anyway. Just know that she's been fitting in real good around here. I'd hate to see her run off because the two of you can't settle your differences."

Cal watched his retreating form and shook his head. What the devil had gone on around here while he'd been gone? Had sweet Marilou spun her web of magic around Chaney's tough old heart, too?

He walked into the kitchen and found the woman in question seated at the table, her hair back in its tidy braid, her face scrubbed and glowing, her eyes closed. At the sound of the screen door slamming, she jumped, startled awake.

"Sorry," he apologized. "Why don't you go up to bed? You can't have gotten much sleep last night."

"I'll be fine. I have work to do today. The garden needs weeding. I haven't had a chance to get to it the past couple of days." As she talked, she went to the oven. She withdrew a plate stacked high with pancakes, ham and eggs and put it on the table.

"I hope it's not ruined," she said, studying it worriedly. "Maybe I should make more."

"This will be just fine," he said, his voice gruffer than he intended, thanks to the lecture he'd just had from Chaney.

When she'd poured him a cup of coffee, he watched her standing indecisively between table and sink. "Sit back down," he said impatiently.

She lifted startled eyes to meet his. "Is anything wrong?"

"We need to talk."

Apparently she didn't like his tone, because she stiffened defensively. "About what?"

"When is this vacation of yours over?"

"The end of next week."

"What are your plans?"

"Plans?"

"Are you going or staying?"

She blinked once, revealing a flicker of hurt, before carefully shuttering her emotions. "I'm not sure there's any reason for me to stay."

"What if I asked you to."

"Why would you do that?" she asked bluntly.

"You're making yourself useful around here."

Her mouth curved ruefully. "Just doing what I'm paid to do."

"You're doing more than that and you know it. I don't want to take advantage, though. If you're planning on staying, we need to think seriously about what you'd do and what your pay would be."

"Cal, you don't need me here," she said with what sounded to him like a trace of wistfulness.

"I never said that."

"I'm not blind. Anybody could do the cooking and cleaning. As for the work I do down in the barn, you could hire a groom in no time. I'm just a rank beginner."

"Do you enjoy it?" he asked, genuinely curious.

The smile that spread across her face was answer enough, but she said, "I'm learning so much. I love being around the horses. I can't wait to see them run. And I've been reading your books. Chaney didn't think you'd mind. Breeding is all so complicated, I mean if you do it right and don't just let nature take its course. And the business side of it, I haven't begun to figure that out yet. What makes a yearling a good investment? It seems to me that it's awfully risky. I saw the story about the spring sales and what you paid for those horses. That's more than I'll earn in my entire lifetime. I had no idea."

Her eyes were shining like polished gemstones. "Do you know what I was reading just last night before Winning Pride had her foal? I think it was in the *General Stud Book* or maybe it was the *Thoroughbred Record*..."

"Hey, slow down," he said, laughing.

"Sorry," she said, grinning apologetically. "I get carried away. I guess I've just been storing all this up, waiting for the right audience. Chaney lets me talk, but I'm not so sure he really listens."

"Oh, I think he's been hearing you loud and clear. I get the feeling he'd like to see you stay on, though he'd never flat-out admit it. What do you really want to do, Marilou?"

"It's not just up to me."

"If it was?"

She hesitated. Finally she lifted her gaze to his. "I don't think it's possible for me to stay on here as an employee, not after the other day. We couldn't go on sleeping down the hall from each other and just ignore the rest. At least I couldn't," she admitted, an embarrassed pink creeping into her cheeks.

Even though he recognized the truth in what she was saying, Cal's heart sank. "There's a lot between us," he agreed. "There's no avoiding that, and I can't promise to keep away from you."

"Then I guess that's our answer." She'd locked her hands together in front of her on the table and sat staring at them. Finally she asked, "What about your grandmother, Cal? I don't want to go home without knowing that's resolved."

"Find her, then," he said softly, overcoming his deep-seated reluctance. "I owe you that much, I guess."

"This is for you, Cal, not me."

Angrily he shoved his chair back from the table. "Don't give me a bunch of psychological babble. Can't you ever leave well enough alone? You're coming out the winner. I've agreed to let you look for her."

"You won't regret it," she vowed, beaming at him in spite of his nasty tone.

"I already do," he said with a heavy sigh. He took one last look at her, then walked out the door.

Chapter Eight

Though she had Cal's blessing to begin the hunt for his grandmother, Marilou recognized that his heart wasn't in the search. Oddly enough, neither was hers. To her surprise, she let the whole day pass without making any attempt to track the old woman down. She blamed her actions on the fact that she had a lot of catching up to do around the house. She'd been so busy helping out with the horses that she'd gotten behind with the gardening and cleaning.

Since the morning air was still cool, she went outside to get the weeding done first. She was kneeling down staring at all the little green shoots in the ground, a frown on her face, when Cal came up behind her.

"Whatever it is, it can't be that serious," he said.

"I'm afraid it is."

"Bugs?"

She shook her head.

"What then?"

"You're going to laugh at me."

He grinned at that. "Actually I could use a good laugh." He hunkered down beside her and stared at the ground. "I don't see the problem." He crumbled a clump of earth between his fingers. "Ground feels good. Everything looks healthy."

"Too healthy," she grumbled.

"Huh?"

"I'm weeding," she said, as if that explained everything. Judging from his blank expression, he still didn't get it. "Cal, I can't tell the weeds from what I planted."

He managed to keep from hooting, but he couldn't suppress the smile that stole across his face. "That's a problem, all right. Haven't you ever done any gardening before?"

She shook her head. "I just figured you'd look at what was coming up and know if it was a good guy or bad one. I mean I planted all these nice, tidy rows, but now it's not so clear to me exactly where they are."

"Maybe you should just let it all run wild and see how it turns out."

She scowled at him. "You are not taking this seriously. And you'd better, because I'm going to leave it in your hands when I go."

He frowned at that, but kept his tone light. "Then we're both in trouble, because I don't know any more about it than you do."

"Well, we're just going to have to learn," she said decisively. "I'll go to the library later and get a book. Or maybe I'll call the nursery and have them send someone over. Do you suppose they make house calls?"

"For the right price, they'll probably talk to the damned plants for you. Call them, if it will make you happy."

He couldn't seem to take his eyes off her face. Finally he reached over and brushed the tip of her nose. "You have a smudge," he explained, his voice dropping. But then his finger moved on to her lips, tracing the curve of her mouth and sending waves of heat through her. She had the most compelling urge to draw that finger deeply into her mouth.

"What am I going to do about you, Marilou?" he said, and she could hear the helplessness and frustration in his tone.

"Kiss me?" she suggested, her breath catching at the instantaneous flaring of desire in his eyes. Maybe if they made love right here in the middle of the garden she could stop worrying about the damned weeds...

He shook his head, ending that fantasy. "Can't do that, sweetheart."

"Why?"

"Because I don't think I could stop with a kiss anymore. I want you too damned much." He caressed her cheek, then swept the pad of his thumb across her lips one last time. Anticipation turned her insides to warm honey, but he was already standing up, already stepping away.

"Cal," she whispered, wishing he didn't have quite such a strong sense of integrity.

"I have to get back to work," he said, looking around desperately as if he hoped Chaney would materialize to rescue him.

"Cal," she said again, but he had already started away and he never looked back.

Marilou blinked back tears of frustration as she turned back to the garden. She still couldn't tell weeds from vegetables, but she yanked up a few sprouts just for the satisfaction of it.

"Oh, hell," she finally muttered. Then she went inside and called the nursery for help.

While she was waiting, she began to clean, spending most of her time in Cal's office. As she was straightening the closet, she came across an old camera, a 35 millimeter that had seen better days. Still, she held it lovingly, focusing it, testing its weight in her hands. Suddenly she desperately wanted to take photographs of everything, especially of Cal. Once she was gone, she would at least have something to remember the adventure by.

Abandoning her chores and forgetting all about the impending arrival of the man from the nursery, she borrowed Chaney's truck and sped into town for film. She spent the rest of the afternoon roaming the farm, shooting pictures of the horses, even capturing Chaney at work, when he wasn't aware of her presence. Roddy, sporting a blush and a shy smile, posed with Devil's Magic. Even Zeke and Pedro paused long enough in their chores for her to get a picture. The only person she missed was Cal. Maybe she was going to have to make do with her memories after all.

That night at dinner, she finally had to admit to herself that she'd spent the day delaying the inevitable. Somehow she had recognized that she and Cal had reached a real turning point. Whatever happened next with his grandmother was going to alter things between them forever. She put the letter in plain view on the kitchen table, then waited for a reaction. Cal's glance kept straying toward the pale blue envelope. His lips settled into a frown and stayed that way.

Finally, when Chaney had gone out after making a snippy remark about escaping the kitchen's icy atmosphere, Cal scowled at her and mumbled, "So?"

Stubbornly Marilou wanted him to say the words. She lifted her gaze to meet his. "I beg your pardon?"

"Don't play games. Did you find her?"

"I haven't started looking," she admitted.

His eyes widened. "Why the hell not?"

"I'm not sure. I didn't get to it." She couldn't bring herself to admit that all day long she'd been depressed by the fact that once Cal's grandmother was found and the two of them were reunited, her role in Cal's life would be at an end.

"Look, I told you it's what I wanted, if that's what's worrying you."

"Maybe I'm still not convinced."

"Sweetheart, I'm not ever going to jump up and down in excitement and plead with you to do this. If that's what you're waiting for, hell will freeze over first."

Marilou sighed. That was exactly what she was hoping for, though she knew better than to admit it. It was entirely likely that Cal would never have—or even want—the sort of warm, loving family relationships that she missed so desperately. Maybe she was the one who was foolish and unrealistic for wanting that for him. He seemed to be perfectly content with the life he'd carved out for himself. Who was she to come along and insist that his quiet, solitary existence needed to be crowded with a grandmother and maybe even the mother and father he'd held in contempt for so long now?

As she debated her right to go on interfering, Cal picked up the letter and studied it, turning it over and over in his hands as if just touching it would reveal something to him. "How're you going to go about finding her?" he asked eventually. "Doesn't seem as if there's a lot to go on. We don't even know her name."

She took his mild curiosity as a good sign, about the most encouragement she was likely to get. "She's your maternal grandmother. We know that much. What was your mother's maiden name?"

"McDonald, I think."

She frowned. Cal apparently caught her disappointment. He said with a rare touch of wry humor,

"You were hoping for something a little more unusual like maybe Capriatti or Janovich?"

Marilou chuckled. "Well, those names probably would be easier to locate in Wyoming, but that's okay. We can still manage."

"What city will you look in?"

"I'll start in Cheyenne, since that's the postmark. Then, if I don't come up with anything, I'll widen the search to the surrounding area. The library probably has phone books. I'll drive over tomorrow and take a look. If worse comes to worst, I'll get a map and just start calling information. The population of the whole state isn't that big."

"That could take forever."

"Be thankful the letter didn't come from New York," she said. "*That* could take forever. This will be a snap. It may cost a little in long-distance call charges, though."

"I don't give a damn about the money. Do what you have to do. What makes you so certain she wants to be found? If she'd really wanted me to find her, wouldn't she have put a phone number or at least an address on the letter?"

"She's old and sick. Remember, she even got your address wrong, and you know some detective probably tracked that down for her. You'd be surprised at how many people are careless about little details. That's why I have a job."

He tossed the letter back onto the table. "Speaking of that, you're probably getting anxious to get back," he said, watching her intently.

"In some ways, I suppose," she said evasively, surprised that there was really very little she missed about the place that had been her home all her life. Already Cal's image was the one that filled her dreams, and his home was beginning to feel like someplace she wanted to belong. That, she reminded herself, was dangerous. Hurriedly she got to her feet and began doing dishes. Suddenly Cal was beside her, dish towel in hand, his heat and scent tempting her.

"I'll dry," he offered.

"There's no need," she said, anxious for him to go, hungry for him to stay.

"I want to."

She shrugged, feigning an indifference that was far from the electric awareness she was actually feeling.

They worked in companionable silence for the next few minutes, though Marilou was aware of an increasing tension in the air. She sensed that it had nothing to do with the letter or Cal's family. She put the last plate in the drainer, rinsed out the sink and started to turn around, only to find herself sandwiched between Cal and the counter. Her gaze shot up to his. Eyes that had darkened to a stormy gray pinned her in place. Warm breath whispered against her cheek.

"Damn, I missed you," he said, the reluctant words sounding as if they'd been wrenched from deep inside him. He brushed a tender kiss across her forehead, then another on her cheek. Marilou felt as if she were suspended in time, holding her breath, anticipating the instant when his lips would finally claim hers with the hunger that she'd never known with anyone but Cal.

"Did you miss me?" he inquired lazily, letting her wait, apparently all too sure that the kiss he withheld was one she wanted all too much. "You said you did this morning. Did you mean it?"

She nodded, feeling too weak and shy and breathless to get the actual words out.

He grinned and sprinkled light, teasing kisses across her shoulder. The sweet torment was every bit as arousing as he'd meant it to be. She swallowed hard as he taunted, "Not good enough, sweetheart. Not nearly good enough."

Something told her that admitting the truth would give Cal an advantage she wasn't nearly ready for him to have. Summoning up a bold and sassy smile, she said sweetly, "Sorry. It's the best I can do on short notice."

As his surprised laughter echoed in the kitchen, she ducked out of his loose embrace and darted for the back door. She made it into the yard before he caught up with her and swung her back into his arms.

"Scaredy-cat," he said softly, holding her close, his hands looped behind her waist, their thighs touching provocatively.

"I'm not the one who ran away to Kentucky," she retorted.

"That was a business trip."

"Of course it was."

"Well, it was."

"Oh, I know that. I also know that it wasn't scheduled to begin until a couple of days later."

"You think that's enough evidence to hang a man on?"

She grinned. "First off, I'm not trying to hang you. And second, that's not my only evidence. I have additional testimony from a very reliable source."

"What source?"

"Joshua Ames. You do consider him reliable, don't you? He is the man you turn to in a crisis?"

A dull red crept into his cheeks, and he avoided her eyes. "What the devil does Joshua have to do with anything?" he grumbled.

"It seems he received some sort of desperation phone call at one in the morning and decided he'd better pay an emergency visit. You'd already fled the danger."

"Joshua was here?"

"You've got it. A nice man, by the way."

"Well, I'll be damned."

"You sound surprised."

"I am. Joshua hasn't set foot on this place since I bought it. He keeps thinking I'll come to my senses and buy a company that actually has offices and skyscrapers or at the very least a secretarial pool."

"I gathered he's not much on wide open spaces."

"Joshua prefers his environment to be regulated by air conditioners and dehumidifiers. If a business can't be computed with a calculator and run by statistics, he figures it isn't worth knowing about. This place is totally beyond him. Every time I send him a bill for hay and oats, he gets heart palpitations. When I told him I wanted to modernize the breeding shed, he thought I'd gone over the edge."

"How did the two of you get to be such friends?"

He looked at her finally, amusement twinkling in his eyes. "He moved in down the block, way back when we were kids. He was frail and sickly then. He wore glasses and liked to study. You can just imagine how the other kids bullied him."

"So you went to his rescue."

"No more than he came to mine in his own way. His house provided a safe haven from the instability at home."

"When he showed up here the other day, he was the one running to the rescue. Judging from the looks of him, he outgrew his need for protection rather dramatically."

Cal drew her closer, regarding her intently. "You thought he was good-looking?" he inquired with a dangerous edge in his voice.

"A hunk, as a matter of fact," she said deliberately.

"And no doubt he thought you were beautiful."

"I believe he did mention finding me attractive," she conceded, then added modestly, "He was probably just being polite."

Cal's fingers tangled in her hair and tightened as his mouth came down on hers. "You won't get polite from me," he murmured just before the hungry demand of his kiss stole their breath away. There was nothing teasing about the hot, moist possessiveness of his mouth covering hers, nothing reluctant about the bold forays of his tongue. Days of wanting and need exploded in that single urgent kiss.

They were both gasping when he finally broke away, and there was a bemused expression in his eyes that she was sure was matched in her own. "God, Marilou," he said raggedly. "What the hell do you do to me?"

"Irritate you?" she suggested, trying for a teasing tone that would deny the thudding of her heart.

He grinned. "Besides that."

"Whatever it is, you seem to have the same effect on me."

"What are we going to do about it?" he asked, sounding surprisingly confused and helpless.

"Give it time, Cal. That's all we can do."

"How much time can we give it if you're going running back to Atlanta in another week or so?"

She leveled a serious look at him and said quietly, "Maybe that's time enough."

He nodded thoughtfully, then that killer smile of his broke across his face. "Who knows? Maybe it is." He took her hand. "Come on."

Startled and still reeling from the implications of their conversation, she gazed at him. "Where?"

"To the barn, my sweet. Where did you think?"

Marilou felt a blush steal over her skin. Cal's smile broadened. "Don't you want to say good-night to Dawn's Magic?"

"Absolutely," she said at once, but she found she had to work very hard to keep the disappointment out of her voice.

* * *

It took Marilou the better part of two days to find Mrs. Caroline Whitfield McDonald. The significance of Cal apparently being named for his grandmother was not lost on her. She began to wonder if his own mother might not be more amenable to a reconciliation than Cal thought.

As she sat daydreaming at the kitchen table, she envisioned a time when this whole house would ring with the sound of laughter and family gossip. Then, daring to take the fantasy one step further, she imagined children underfoot. Hers and Cal's. Those stubborn, willful little devils, who would charm and torment, just like their father. She sighed. It was a wonderful dream, but that's all it was. If she doubted that for an instant, Cal's reaction to her news proved just how wide the gap between fantasy and reality really was.

She found him standing by the rail at the training track, watching as one of the new two-year-olds worked out. His gaze was so intent, he didn't even notice when she came up alongside him. He held a stopwatch in his hand and kept his eyes glued to the horse as it moved around the near turn. When the new chestnut colt flew by, he nodded in satisfaction.

"A good workout?" she asked.

He turned then without surprise and she realized he had known she was there after all. "Better than good. That horse could be on the track in Miami or New York before the end of the summer. He'll certainly be ready for the Derby prep races next spring."

He waved the jockey over and questioned him extensively about the way the horse had run. Marilou listened closely, anxious to learn everything she could about the training process. Her fascination with the business was growing daily, as was her desire to capture more of the excitement on film. After that one day, she'd put Cal's camera back where she'd found it and tucked the film in her suitcase. She hadn't dared to take it out again. It had stirred too many longings, reminded her of too many plans long since abandoned.

Cal turned back to her just then and apparently some of her wistfulness was written on her face. "What's wrong?" he asked at once.

"I was just wishing I'd brought my camera down here."

"Good heavens," he teased. "What's a tourist without a camera?"

When she didn't smile at his lighthearted banter, he sobered at once. "What am I missing here?"

"Nothing."

He touched her cheek, the stroke of his finger gentle. "Marilou?"

"It's just that photography was once very important to me."

"That's the career you gave up?"

She nodded. "If you call it a career when I never did a day's work in it."

"You studied it in college, though?"

"Yes. I even won a couple of contests. My portfolio was very impressive, according to some of the professors I had."

"What had you planned to do? Studio work? Photojournalism?"

"I hadn't really decided. That was one of the reasons I wanted so badly to go to Europe. I thought maybe I'd be able to figure out over there whether I had the talent to do photographic essays, gallery showings." She grinned ruefully. "I guess you can see why my parents thought it was risky. My ambition was to do the extraordinary. I'm not sure whether the talent lived up to the dream. Even if it had, there were no guarantees I could turn it into a paying career."

"And your folks didn't want you to be a starving artist?"

"Especially not way off in Europe all alone."

"Couldn't you find a compromise?"

"Maybe if we hadn't gotten so angry we could have. As it turned out, we never had the chance to try."

Cal touched her cheek. "I'm sorry."

"Thanks."

"If you miss it so much, why don't you start over now? You're hardly too old to be launching a new career."

She shrugged. "Maybe I'm just too scared. I hadn't touched a camera in years until I borrowed yours the other day. I've gotten used to playing it safe. You can't fail if you don't try."

"I know all about playing it safe," he said gently. "And as someone very wise reminded me recently, it may not be the best way to live your life, not if you expect to find real happiness."

Uncomfortable with the still-sensitive topic, she was glad for the opening to change the subject. "Speaking of risks and moving forward, I found your grandmother."

Cal's expression altered at once, as if he'd automatically slammed the door on his emotions, which only seconds before had been laid bare. "Where?" he said, his voice tight.

"She lives on a cattle ranch about seventy-five miles north of Cheyenne. Seems she's pretty well-known around those parts. I spoke to the editor of the weekly paper in the closest town, and he says she's been sick for months now, but she's still running that ranch—essentially by herself. I guess that stubborn streak is definitely a family trait, just like she said."

"I guess you're relieved, knowing that she's still alive, that we're not too late."

"Aren't you?"

"I suppose."

She had to fight the desire to snap at him for his callousness. She said only, "I've got the phone number up at the house. With the time difference, it's still too early to call, but maybe when you come in for lunch?"

He shoved his hands in his pockets and stared at her, his expression as forbidding as she'd ever seen it. "I'm not calling," he said emphatically.

"I don't understand," Marilou said, her voice faltering as she studied his implacable expression. "You promised, Cal."

"I said to find her. I never once said what I would do once you had."

Marilou felt disappointment and fury stirring inside her. She was tired of playing games when she couldn't begin to understand the tough, insensitive rules. She shoved her hands in her pockets and faced Cal squarely. "You know something, Cal Rivers, Joshua was right about you. You are nothing but a lily-livered coward."

"What?" he demanded, obviously stunned by the angry charge.

"You heard me. You are so flat-out terrified of being hurt that you don't give a flying fig how much you hurt other people. Your parents. Your grandmother. Me. Not a one of us matters to you as long as you can go on living the way you want to. You like being alone so you don't have to be responsible for anyone but yourself. Talk about safe! You're so safe shut away out here that you might as well be locked up in some jail cell. If you ask me, it's a hell of a way to live."

"It suits me," he said stonily.

"I guess it does, but it doesn't suit me. I've done my part. I tried to help you. I've found your grandmother. I'll pack my things and be out of here in the morning."

Even as the angry words tumbled out of her mouth, she realized that saying goodbye would be the hardest thing she'd ever done. With unexpected clarity, she saw what had happened the past few weeks. Like some silly schoolgirl, she'd gone and fallen in love with Cal Rivers, the most impossible, contrary man on the face of the earth. On the one hand, he represented the kind of bold, self-confident adventurer she'd always dreamed about; on the other, he was the antithesis of the family man she needed to feel whole.

Well, maybe she couldn't undo what she was feeling, but she could sure as hell walk away from it before she got her heart broken. She'd get over him eventually. All she would have to do would be to keep reminding herself what a self-centered coward he was. No woman with a brain left in her head could love a man like that for long.

She looked into his face one last time and tried to interpret the riot of emotions in his eyes. Whatever he was thinking, though, he was staying silent. That silence, confirming all of her most damning thoughts, was enough finally to send her packing.

She whirled around and ran back to the house, desperate to escape, even more desperate to keep Cal from seeing the hot, bitter tears that spilled down her cheeks.

Chapter Nine

Cal didn't go near the house the rest of the afternoon. He didn't think he could stand to see that awful, defeated look in Marilou's eyes again. He'd seen her bitter disappointment, but he'd been unable to say the words that would make it go away. Every time he'd tried, they'd stuck in his throat. A simple yes would have done it, but even that was beyond him.

Besides, nothing about this was simple. Feelings buried for so long weren't easy to put into words. Maybe he was a fool or a coward or both, but he wouldn't be a hypocrite to boot. He couldn't feign enthusiasm just to please Marilou. Though he credited her with being intuitive about most things, she didn't understand this. She couldn't possibly realize what she was asking of him. He didn't want to go back, didn't want to dredge up all of the old hurts. What possible difference could it make at this late date for him to go barging into the life of a woman he'd never met?

It was past supper time when he finally got up the courage to walk into the house. With a sense of resignation, he saw that Marilou wasn't in the kitchen where he'd grown used to finding her. There were no dishes on the table, no pots simmering on the stove, no wonderful aromas coming from the oven.

Not that he was hungry. He doubted if he could get food past the lump that was lodged in his throat. He just wanted her to be there, waiting for him with that gentle, trusting, caring smile. Instead the room felt cold and empty without her. He was getting a taste of what his life would be like without her.

Logic told him he could make everything right in a heartbeat. All he had to do was admit he was wrong and say he'd make the stupid phone call. Maybe he wouldn't even have to make it. Maybe the promise would be enough to buy a few more days.

A few more days to do what? Convince her that family wasn't all that important? Not likely. To Marilou, who'd lost her only relatives so tragically, it was obviously the only thing that did matter. It was the one blind spot in her otherwise open-minded nature.

Still, even knowing this was something that would always put them at loggerheads, he couldn't let her go. He knew that as surely as he'd always known when it was time to move on, time to hunt for a new challenge. Right now he felt settled, and he intended to keep it that way. Marilou, he'd come to realize, was a major part of that feeling of contentment that had swept over him so unexpectedly when he'd bought Silver River Stables. The feeling of finally finding his niche had grown stronger day by day ever since. One thing life had taught him was that when something was good, you reached for it and held on for as long as the ride lasted. Well, this was one ride that was a long way from over.

There was one way he could buy himself some time, he decided, though he felt a twinge of regret at the duplicity of it. She couldn't leave without his say-so. She'd returned her rental car after the first week. Since then she'd borrowed his car or Chaney's old pickup to run errands. She actually seemed to prefer that dented, rusty four-by-four. He'd watched her speeding up the drive, noisily shifting gears with more enthusiasm than skill, the brim of her Atlanta Braves baseball cap shading her eyes, which he knew instinctively were flashing with excitement.

Her pure, full-throttle way of attacking life, which he had a feeling she'd been holding in check for too long now, was one of the things he'd come to like most about her. She tackled new projects with the same determination that he brought to learning a new business. He'd never known a woman to get so much enjoyment out of the craziest things. Mucking out the damned stalls, for instance. Weeding the vegetable garden she'd planted outside the kitchen door. Getting up at the crack of dawn to make homemade biscuits and laughing when the first batch turned out to be as hard and heavy as bricks. Damn, he was going to miss her genuine zest for life. How could he possibly let her go?

The fact was he couldn't, not unless he was the worst sort of fool. And if he refused to give her a lift into town or to let Chaney take her, she'd have to stick around so they could work things out. In his desperation, he refused to consider how unlikely it would be that a woman essentially being held hostage would bargain with the man doing the kidnapping. He simply went to bed with his strategy set and his mind made up.

He wasn't expecting his plan to be foiled, but he stayed awake the whole night, just in case she took it into her head to sneak out. He was already in the kitchen drinking coffee—lousy coffee, now that he'd gotten used to hers—when she came downstairs at daybreak, lugging her suitcase. The sight of that bag made his heart ache, so he concentrated on her instead.

She was dressed for travel, as neat and tidy as the day she'd arrived in that beguiling oversize T-shirt and jeans that fit snugly over a fanny that was beginning to drive him crazy. She'd swept her hair up in a top knot and jammed her baseball cap over it. Stray wisps teased at her cheeks. When one strand fell into her eyes, she blew it away with lips tinted a tantalizing shade of strawberry pink. He felt his heart turn over in his chest and the now-familiar lump formed swiftly in his throat. His blood turned hot and sizzled with uncompromised lust.

Without saying a word, without even looking at him, she poured herself a cup of coffee and stood at the counter. Her gaze was directed out the window. Everything about her stance spelled angry distance, feisty determination and hurry. It was evident she couldn't wait to get away.

"You can at least sit at the table with me," he grumbled, his whole body screaming for some slight contact, one fleeting brush of flesh against flesh.

"I'd rather not," she said primly.

"Oh, for heaven's sake, Marilou—"

She whipped her head around and her expression stopped the remainder of his explosion. "I'll be leaving as soon as Chaney's free to take me."

"Chaney won't be free," he said, and his chin jutted just as defiantly as hers.

She blinked and for just a second looked uncertain. "What . . . what do you mean? I spoke with him last night."

"And I spoke to him after that. I sent him to Miami to talk to a trainer down there."

She traded uncertainty for immediate indignation. "You what?" she demanded, her coffee cup hovering midway between her mouth and the counter. "How am I supposed to leave?"

He tilted his chair back and smiled complacently. "I guess you'll just have to wait until he gets back. Could be tomorrow. Could be next week. It's hard to tell."

The complacency was obviously a mistake. Her cup hit the counter so hard the coffee splattered every which way. "In a pig's eye," she said, planting hands on hips. "I said I was leaving today and I am."

"It's a long walk to town."

"Roddy will take me."

"Not if he hopes to keep his job."

Fresh indignation brought a flush to her cheeks. "You wouldn't."

The front legs of his chair hit the floor emphatically. "I would," he said grimly.

"But that's rotten. In fact, that's blackmail."

"That's management. With Chaney away, we all have extra work to do around here. You could help out, in fact."

"Go to hell," she snapped furiously. "You know that has nothing to do with it. You don't need me and you could spare Roddy for the half hour or so it would take to get me to town."

"I've been to hell," he said evenly. "I prefer it here. As for my reasoning, you can accept it or not. It won't change anything."

"You are the most arrogant, maddening man it has ever been my misfortune to meet. If it weren't for the fact that your grandmother wants so badly to meet you, I'd say she's better off not knowing what you're really like."

"Thanks," he said. "Now, if you'll excuse me, I have work to do."

He was chuckling when he walked out the door. He was not laughing an hour later when he happened to glance up and see Marilou walking down the driveway, struggling with her suitcase. Another two or three minutes and she'd be at the highway. In her present mood, she probably wouldn't hesitate to hitch a ride.

"Dammit," he muttered and took off at a run. Chaney's pickup was closest. Fortunately the keys were above the visor. He cranked up the reluctant engine and took off down the drive, slamming on the brakes in a cloud of dust when he came alongside her.

"Get in," he shouted over the rumble of the engine.

She didn't even spare him a glance. He could see her lips moving as she muttered something that sounded like, "Not on your life."

"Marilou, get in this truck." His voice was no doubt loud enough by now to be heard in the far paddocks.

"Who died and made you king of the road?"

He counted to ten, as the truck heaved and sputtered, reluctantly keeping pace with her slow steps. "Marilou, please. You can't walk all the way to town," he reasoned. "It's miles, and there's a storm threatening."

"I'm sure someone will come along and give me a lift."

"If they don't rape or murder you."

"I can protect myself."

"Can you really?" he countered with a weary smile. He drew in a deep breath then and said what he probably should have said the day before. "Okay, sweetheart," he said with a certain sense of inevitability. "You win."

"Win?"

"Yes, win, dammit. You might as well stick around for the grand finale of all your meddling."

That brought her to a stop at last. She dropped her suitcase, turned and looked at him. "What grand finale?" she inquired, her voice still thick with skepticism.

"You and I are going to fly to Wyoming," he said, improvising. He figured such drastic measures were the only way to convince her of his sincerity. He could tell that right now she wasn't much in the mood to trust any promise that fell short of total capitulation.

Her eyes widened at the announcement. "Wyoming?" she repeated as if it were on the moon and getting there was nigh on to impossible.

When she added weakly, "Together," he knew he had her hooked. He had also landed himself in one helluva mess. A trip to Wyoming held about as much appeal to him as falling into a bed of nettles.

"Together," he confirmed wearily, wondering what it would take to bribe the pilot to land them in some remote stretch of Montana and abandon them there. Maybe after he'd made wild, passionate love to her for a week or so, she'd forget all about his grandmother. Maybe he'd forget that the fact that she cared was why he needed her in his life.

"Why are you changing your mind? What made you decide to go to Wyoming?"

To get you to stay in my life, he wanted to say, but stubborn pride silenced him. Instead he said, "If I call the woman out of the blue the way you want me to, she'd probably die of shock. The more I think about it, the more I see that going out there is the only thing to do. We might as well get it over with.''

"Together?" Marilou said again.

Her expression, caught between excitement and panic, made Cal smile despite his many misgivings. "What's the matter, Marilou? Scared of flying?"

"No, of course not," she denied hotly.

"Then it must be me, after all."

She shot him a determined look. "Not a chance."

"Then you'll come along?"

A smile broke across her face, and Cal felt the dread that had filled him for the past twenty-four hours finally begin to abate. "I wouldn't miss it for the world," she said, clambering awkwardly into the truck. "When do we leave?"

"As long as your bags are already packed," he said dryly, "I suppose we might as well try to get my plane fueled and ready by this afternoon."

As soon as he'd uttered the words, his own desperate panic set in, but he had only to look at the radiance of Marilou's expression to see that he'd done the only thing he could possibly do.

Though she wanted to follow Cal upstairs to make sure he actually packed a bag and didn't sneak off to Timbuktu, Marilou settled down at the kitchen table to wait. She drank another cup of the awful coffee that Cal had made that morning. It left her already-jangled nerves even more frayed. It finally got so bad she couldn't make herself sit still. She began to pace. Then she began throwing a load of laundry into the washer. Then she wiped off the countertops again.

How had her life become so complicated? She was about to go chasing off across the country to the Wild West with a man who was as close as she was ever likely to come to a free-spirited cowboy, a man she wanted so badly her whole body ached with longing.

"Good grief," she murmured. She felt Cal's touch at the nape of her neck, setting off sparks low in her abdomen.

"Are you okay?" he asked worriedly.

"Fine."

"We don't have to go," he volunteered so quickly that she smiled.

"Oh, no, you don't. I'm not letting you off the hook that easily."

He grinned ruefully. "It was worth a try."

"And a noble try it was. Where's the plane?"

"At the airport. The pilot's having it refueled. Chaney will take us. He should be here any minute."

"Chaney?" she said, her eyes widening incredulously. "I thought he was in Miami."

"Don't look at me like that. He was. He came back with the plane just now. I can't go off and leave this place without someone being in charge."

"If you say so," she said doubtfully.

"I swear to you that I did not have him hidden in the barn."

"If he arrives here smelling like manure, you're going to have a lot of explaining to do, Cal Rivers."

"If he shows up smelling like anything else, *he's* going to have a lot of explaining to do. He was supposed to be down there hanging around the Gulfstream backstretch talking to trainers."

A few minutes later when Chaney pulled up in front of the house, Cal took their bags out.

"How'd the trip go?"

"The plane ride was just great. I wasn't on the ground long enough to get much business done, though. I'd barely made it to the track when you called and said to get home. What the devil's the danged emergency?"

"I'm going to Wyoming."

"What's out there?"

"Family business."

Chaney seemed to take count of the bags. "She going too?"

"Yes. We shouldn't be gone more than a day or two."

The old man got a speculative gleam in his eyes. "You stay as long as you want," he said slyly. "The boys and I can manage around here."

"A couple of days," Cal repeated adamantly. "This isn't a vacation."

"Maybe it ought to be," Chaney countered, casting a pointed look at Marilou. "If a man's got any sense at all, he ought to take advantage of the opportunities that come his way."

"Thanks for the advice," Cal said dryly, avoiding Marilou's gaze.

* * *

It was only later, when the plane was in the air, that she dared to meet Cal's eye. "Opportunity, huh?"

"I don't think he meant that the way it sounded," he said, but he was watching her speculatively. The hungry longing in his eyes turned her blood to liquid fire. Her heart pounded with sweet anticipation.

"I think he did," she said, her voice husky. "When did Chaney turn matchmaker?"

"You said it yourself. He's hooked on those blueberry muffins you've been baking for him. He's not above any sneaky tactic in the book that'll get you to stick around."

Deep in her gut she felt the first stirring of real hope. Chaney's approval meant a lot. If she could win over a crusty old dyed-in-the-wool bachelor like him, surely she had a chance to gain Cal's trust and love. She had no doubts at all that he was attracted to her. The frequent flaring of desire in his eyes was plain as day. Even his most casual touches were meant to inflame and entice. And they were effective. Half the time she felt as if her heart was hammering so hard it would burst right through her chest.

She looked up and realized he was watching her with that familiar look in his eyes. He held out his hand and she placed hers in it.

"Scared?" he asked.

She shook her head. "Excited. I can't believe I'm doing this. I've never done anything this impulsively in my life."

"You came to Florida."

"True."

"And you moved in with me."

"I didn't actually move in with you."

"Oh?"

"I mean I moved into your house, temporarily, but that's different from moving in with you the way you mean."

"How did I mean it?"

"Stop it, Cal. You're deliberately teasing me."

He grinned. "I suppose. I was hoping I was doing more than that."

She eyed him warily. "Did you lure me out here to try to seduce me?"

"Sweetheart, I could have done that back in Florida," he said with irritating but all too accurate arrogance.

"Says who?"

He grinned and rubbed his thumb in erotic circles in her palm. His gaze held hers and he said softly, "Says me."

She swallowed hard. "Okay, so maybe you could," she said breezily. "The point is that we are going to Wyoming so that you can meet your grandmother. There won't be enough time for dalliance."

He hooted at that. "Dalliance?"

"Cal Rivers, if you keep laughing at me, any prospect for kisses now or at any time in the future is seriously jeopardized."

"Is that so?"

"Yes, that's so," she began, but her breath caught as he lowered his lips to hers. The kiss began before she could think to stop it. It went on because she didn't want to end the glorious sensations that swept through her as his mouth moved against hers.

"Damn you," she murmured, when he deliberately lifted his head for one taunting instant. The victory was clearly his. She caught Cal's triumphant laughter as she covered his lips with her own. She was unprepared for the sheer exhilaration of those kisses, for the deliciously wicked freedom she felt even as he was binding her heart to his. Even after they were on the ground in Cheyenne, Marilou's heart was still somewhere in the clouds.

When Cal registered them in a one-bedroom suite at an old hotel in Cheyenne, she was fully aware of the implications. When he ordered champagne with their dinner from room service, her pulse soared. And when he slid his arms around her, neither of them gave a thought to the meal that was being ruined while they discovered the sensual adventure of being together.

Chapter Ten

"Do you have any idea how incredible I feel?" Marilou said, freeing herself from Cal's embrace and spinning around in the wonderful, old-fashioned suite with its Victorian furniture and red brocade draperies. It was luxurious and slightly decadent, sending her imagination off on a delicious fantasy. She'd had no idea her thoughts could turn so wicked. It was clear that Cal brought out this deeply feminine and sensual side of her.

Oh, my, how she intended to enjoy it! She was here in a new and exciting place with a man she loved, a man who just might be coming to care for her. All of the pieces of her life—the longing for adventure, the search for romance, the need for family—all of it seemed to be suddenly falling into place. It was as if she'd waited her whole life for this man, for this moment. The sweet throb of anticipation made her giddy.

Then the thought of Cal's grandmother stole in and sobered her at once.

"Cal, shouldn't we go to your grandmother's ranch?"

"Not tonight. It's already late. Besides we deserve this time just for us."

"You're not just putting off the inevitable, are you?"

"No. I want you, sweetheart, and I can't wait any longer to have you. I intend to do a little long-delayed romancing before we get side-tracked."

"Champagne. Chateaubriand for two. That's definitely romantic. Isn't that outrageously expensive?" she asked.

"You're worth it," he murmured, reaching for her, his gaze still smoky with desire. "Do you have any idea how beautiful you are?"

"Beautiful? Me?"

Cal laughed and drew her close. The musky scent of his after-shave enticed her and the last guilty thoughts of Cal's grandmother fled.

"Don't play coy. You know you're gorgeous, especially the way you look now with your red hair spilling loose over your shoulders and your cheeks all flushed." He ran his fingers through the silky tangles. "You look like a woman who was made for loving."

The huskiness of his voice and the gleam in his eyes made her knees go weak. This was the way love was supposed to feel, terrific and scary all at once. It was supposed to set free all your wildest dreams. It allowed you to dare, to take impossible risks, trusting that love would keep you safe.

"Cal," she said tentatively, her imagination flying again.

"Hmm?"

She stood on tiptoe and whispered in his ear, "I have this fantasy."

For an instant, he appeared stunned. Then he immediately sat down, crossed his legs and assumed a look of total fascination. "Yeah? What sort of fantasy does an innocent young lady from Atlanta have?"

"You won't laugh?"

"Sweetheart," he said fervently. "If this is leading where I think it's leading, I definitely will not laugh."

She grinned, thoroughly emboldened by his enthusiasm and maybe just a little by the champagne. "I think maybe it came from watching too many Westerns. You know, the cowboy was always coming into some bar, hot and dusty from the trail. And this woman was always dressed up real fancy and the room always looked a little like this."

"Like a bordello?"

"You're catching on."

"My, my. I never would have guessed where your thoughts would roam. In this fantasy of yours, is the woman, shall we say, an employee? Or is she a lady who's just arrived from back east?"

"I think she'd better be a lady," she said, blushing furiously as Cal's gaze lingered on her meaningfully. If he'd actually stripped away her clothes, she could have felt no more exposed or wanted or vulnerable. "I don't have the experience for the other."

"In this game, imagination is almost as important as skill. So far, believe me, you're at the top of the class. Tell me, in this fantasy does the cowboy offer to buy the lady a drink?"

She nodded. "Champagne, of course."

"Of course. Fortunately this cowboy happens to have a bottle handy." He poured a refill of the sparkling liquid into a crystal flute and handed it to her, their fingers grazing. His eyes caught hers and held until her pulse bucked, then raced faster than any Thoroughbred in his stables. He poured a glass for himself, then touched his glass to hers. Even the ping of crystal meeting crystal made her senses sing.

"To fantasy," he said.

"To fantasy," she murmured, thinking that the reality was already surpassing the excitement of the dream.

"Marilou," he whispered, his voice a low command that drew her gaze back to his.

Eyes wide with anticipation, she waited.

"I think we need to pick up the pace of this fantasy, before I go crazy here."

"What happens next in your version?" she said.

"I thought this was your fantasy."

"Actually, I sort of run out of steam when they get to the top of the steps," she admitted regretfully.

He swallowed hard and stared at her. "Are you..."

"Yep. Afraid so."

"I guess I knew that. Are you sure this is what you want, then?"

She nodded slowly, her gaze never leaving his. "More than anything. But you're going to have to take over from here. I'm out of lines."

A lazy, provocative smile spread across his face. "I think I can manage. It seems to me that the next scene definitely calls for a kiss."

"A chaste kiss?"

"Absolutely," he said, drawing her down on his lap and brushing his lips across her forehead. She sighed and settled in his arms, her fingers stroking the faint stubble on his cheeks. He went absolutely still at her touch, his gaze leveled on her face.

"And then?" she whispered.

"And then a not so chaste kiss," he said, his voice rough as sandpaper and so low she had to lean close to hear it. The scent of warm musk enveloped her.

The first kiss with its merest whisper of danger brought her to the edge of a precipice. The second pushed her over the edge into a riot of glorious new sensations. He gently brushed aside her hair and caressed the exposed sweep of sensitive skin, murmuring endearments all the while, intent on easing fears she'd long since overcome. When he unfastened the first button of her blouse, she felt daring. When he undid the rest, she felt a rush of heat and the slow, sweet tug of longing.

"Touch me," he pleaded, and she skimmed cautious fingers over skin that was already on fire to her touch. The textures, so different from her own, fascinated her, and with his encouragement she became increasingly bold, stripping away his shirt, anxiously tugging off the T-shirt beneath. Back in Florida she'd seen him in no more, seen him with his bronzed shoulders bared to the sun, but there she hadn't been able to touch. Now she couldn't seem to satisfy herself with one caress. She wanted to stroke, to savor, to taste. She wanted to stare until she'd memorized every fascinating, masculine inch of him.

The cowboy of her fantasy was even sexier in flesh and blood. And he was willing. Even an innocent virgin could tell the man was hot and bothered. Her fingers toyed with his belt buckle and she could feel his stomach muscles rippling and tensing. His sharp intake of breath stilled her hands when they dared to roam lower still.

"I like touching you," she admitted, suddenly shy and all too aware of the sensual power the man held over her. No gentleman would take advantage of that power. Besides, this was Cal and, for all his flaws, she loved him. She'd been telling him exactly what was on her mind from the day they'd met. There was no sane reason to stop now. When she dared to look at him, she saw that he was far from shocked by her statement. If anything, the tenderness in his eyes was deeper than before.

"No more than I like looking at you," he said. "And holding you. And touching you." His hand gently cupped her breast. The sight of tanned flesh against cream skin was erotic enough, but his thumb deliberately taunted her nipple until jolts of excitement shot through her. She gasped at the intensity of sensation.

"Scared?" he inquired with gentle concern.

"Only of not living up to your expectations."

"There's no chance in hell of that. The only way you could disappoint me now would be to call this off."

"I don't think I could do that if I wanted to," she said as the tension mounted to an unbearable level. Whether the timing was right or not, she wanted this, and she sensed that Cal needed it. He needed to know that she trusted him, that he could count on her no matter how the next few days turned out. She wanted desperately to be there for him, in every way that a woman supported a man she loved.

"Don't make me wait any longer, Marilou. Let me love you."

"I want that, Cal. I really want that," she whispered as he swept her up and carried her into the bedroom.

After that, fantasy and reality became a glorious blur. Sensations she'd only read about soared through her, leaving her body trembling and her heart filled with joy. Cal was gentle and passionate and demanding, branding her as his own forever. No matter what happened from this moment on, she would be his, body and soul. She had given him an emotional part of herself that she could never reclaim, and she had given it without regret.

As ecstasy faded, though, and Cal lay by her side, she was less certain whether he had shared himself as fully with her as it had seemed. Though he had withheld nothing in terms of tenderness or explosive passion, he had distanced himself almost at once. Even though he continued to hold her close, his expression was shuttered now, his mood increasingly withdrawn, his silence almost palpable. It was as if a chill had crept into the room, a chill that no amount of body heat could warm. To her dismay, Marilou felt far lonelier than she had before they'd made love. Instead of binding them together as she'd hoped, the act of love seemed to have set them adrift.

Cal felt as if he'd been poleaxed.

No woman had ever affected him as deeply, had ever loved him as unselfishly as Marilou had. Her willingness to give scared the dickens out of him. He should have known better. His life was complicated enough without getting entangled with an inexperienced woman who was bound to make more of this than she should. How the hell could he explain *that* to her, though? Just about anything honest he could think of to say would devastate her. He couldn't bring himself to lie.

So he stayed silent, holding her, knowing that with each passing minute she was getting more confused, more hurt.

Finally she shivered and sat up, pulling the blankets around her.

"Cold?" Cal asked. "Want me to turn up the heat?"

Marilou shook her head. "I'd rather you told me what's wrong."

He felt ice, where only moments ago there had been fire. He searched for glib words and found only evasions. "Wrong?" he said, feeling like a damned fool. "I don't know what you mean."

His hand continued to caress her thigh in an attempt to reassure her in some way. She brushed it aside and slid away from him. The movement put inches between them. It might as well have been a mile.

"Cal, less than five minutes ago you and I were as close as two people can possibly be. Now I feel as if we're on different planets."

"It was great sex," he blurted. The crude words were out before he could censor them, the damage done.

She stared at him in shock for no longer than a heartbeat. Then her temper kicked in. "Great sex!" she repeated furiously, getting out of bed and dragging the blankets with her. She kicked the surplus out of the way as if it were the train of an elegant gown. It was an impressive performance. If it hadn't been for the welling of tears in her eyes, she might have convinced him that she was more angry than hurt, more furious than confused. She did try, though. Oh, how she tried!

"Great sex! You have one helluva nerve."

Cal knew that his cheeks had turned a dull red. He used her anger to increase the distance until he felt safer. It didn't seem to matter that he also felt like slime. "What were you expecting?" he mocked, deliberately undercutting the very real ties he couldn't bear to acknowledge. "Undying commitment? You know how I feel about commitment. I've never lied to you about that."

"No. I'll give you that. You've been honest. You've always made it plain that you don't ever intend to think about anybody other than yourself. I guess I just fooled myself into thinking that you might be changing. This trip..." She waved her hand at the bed. "This . . . I thought it meant something."

"It does," he said in a voice that had gone whisper soft, desperate.

"What?" When he remained stoically silent, she said, "Answer me, dammit. What does this mean? Maybe 'great sex' says it all. If so, just say it."

"I don't know," he exploded. "Okay? I don't know what it means. You've taken me by surprise."

She stared at him, clearly stunned. "I've taken you by surprise? Cal, as naive as I may be, even I have seen this coming for weeks."

"I'm not just talking about the sex. I'm talking about all of it, whatever all of it is. Don't push, Marilou. Too much is happening right now and I need time to think about it."

She drew herself up proudly. He gave her credit for withstanding his cruel assault with dignity. She'd never looked more beautiful than she did as she wrapped the blanket more tightly around her and grabbed a pillow from the bed. "Well, when you figure it out," she said softly, "I'll be in the other room."

"Fine."

"Fine."

But it wasn't fine, Marilou thought miserably as she tried to find a comfortable position on the hard, cramped Victorian-style sofa. Cal had betrayed her trust in the most devastating way possible. He'd lured her out here under false pretenses: he'd only come to pacify her. For all she knew he didn't have any intention of going to see his grandmother in the morning. The sex had probably just been a delaying tactic. He was such a skilled and imaginative lover, he'd probably figured he could keep her occupied until she forgot all about the reason for the trip.

Well, the delays were over. It was time to fish or cut bait. This wasn't something he needed to do for her. It was something he had to do for himself. If only she could make him see that. She spent the rest of the night trying to come up with some way to get through that impenetrable defensive shield of his. Not one single bright idea occurred to her. Not even one *lousy* idea presented itself. The only thing she got for her sleepless night on the sofa was a stiff neck.

She had already ordered coffee and toast from room service by the time he ventured out of the bedroom in the morning. She felt some satisfaction when she noted that he looked just about as rotten as she felt.

"Sleep well?" he inquired, regarding her warily as he poured himself a cup of coffee.

"Well enough. You?"

"Terrific. Like a baby, in fact."

"There's toast if you want it."

"I'll go down for breakfast as soon as I've showered."

"Fine."

"You're welcome to come along."

"That's all right. The toast is plenty."

"Fine."

"Cal..."

"Marilou..."

"You first."

"I'm sorry about last night," he said roughly. "I suppose I managed to make the whole thing sound cheap, and that's not the way I felt about it at all."

"I'm sorry if I assumed too much." She had to force the words out. It hurt to admit she'd been wrong. It hurt to accept that they would never be more deeply involved than they had been last night. Casual lovers. The phrase, about as contradictory as any two words she could imagine, made her want to throw up.

"I guess we're just going to have to slow down," Cal said, looking nervous as a teenager trying to explain his way out of a first sexual encounter. "We don't seem to operate on the same wavelength when it comes to this. I thought you were ready, but obviously I was wrong."

"After today it won't really matter," she said stiffly. "Once you've seen your grandmother, I'll be going back to Atlanta. I'll be out of your hair and you can go on with your life any way that suits you."

His expression hardened at her matter-of-fact tone. "Right."

For one fleeting second, she thought she detected a chink in his armor, a hint of longing. "That is what you want, isn't it?"

He hid whatever he was really feeling behind a wall of stubborn pride. "That's exactly what I want. And you can't wait to get back to Atlanta, right?"

She sighed in resignation and said what he wanted to hear. "Right."

Wrong, Marilou thought dejectedly as he slammed out of the room. It was all turning out wrong.

Except for the visit to Cal's grandmother. At least that would be a happy ending. He hadn't backed out of it. She found him downstairs in the coffee shop, sipping black coffee and puffing on a cigarette. It was the first time she'd caught him smoking since she'd first arrived at his house in Florida. She scowled at the number of half-smoked butts he had already ground out in the ashtray. When he spotted her, he put out the one he'd been holding and regarded her balefully.

"No comment?"

She shook her head. "You're a grown man. If you want to ruin your lungs, it's up to you."

"It's hard to believe there's something about my life about which you don't hold a strong opinion."

"Don't kid yourself. I have an opinion. I just see no point in sharing it."

"Damn," he muttered, crumpling up the remainder of the pack and tossing it on the table. He scowled at her fiercely. "I knew you were trouble the day I met you."

She swallowed hard at the anger she heard in his voice. "I never meant to be, Cal. I came because of the letter. I thought it was the right thing to do. Now I just want what's best for you."

"And you've got it all figured out what that is? It must be nice to go through life being so sure of things."

"This morning I'm not sure about much."

"See, there you go again."

"All I said . . ."

"I know what you said, and I know what you meant," he snapped irritably. "Oh, for heaven's sake, sit down."

"What a pleasant invitation," she retorted, but she sat. "What time are you planning to drive out to your grandmother's?"

"We might as well go now," he said with such sullen indifference that she wanted to pour his steaming hot coffee straight into his miserable lap.

"I thought you wanted breakfast," she said instead.

"I'd rather get this over with."

"You make it sound like some sort of torture."

"That's exactly what it feels like."

Cal's black mood didn't lift on the long drive to his grandmother's ranch, despite the fact that the sky was a brilliant blue and the scenery was spectacular. Even though Marilou longed once more for her camera so she could record the uncommonly desolate beauty, she found that the setting was only a minor distraction from the tension in the air. Cal made no attempt at small talk, and Marilou's own feeble tries were greeted with stony silence.

How could he be like this, when he was about to meet his grandmother? she wondered. She would have been on pins and needles with excitement instead of wallowing in this miserable attitude of dread. This difference between them was something so basic she should have accepted long ago how unsuited they were. It was possible for two people in love to overcome differences in life-styles, but not conflicting values that went to the very core of their personalities. How could she have been blind enough to fall in love with a man who didn't treasure family the way she did?

It was nearly noon when Cal turned onto the long road leading from the highway to his grandmother's ranch. Despite his glowering expression, she was almost certain she saw a glimmer of interest in his eyes as he scanned the property. Though the holdings seemed to be vast, there were signs of disrepair. His frown deepened as they passed a crumbling fence post.

"I suppose it's difficult for her to stay on top of everything if she's been ill," Marilou ventured.

"I suppose."

"How big do you think the ranch is?"

"How would I know?"

She shrugged. "The house looks like it's been taken care of," she said as the long, low structure finally came into view. It had fresh white paint and black trim. Huge planters of pink and purple flowers bordered the front steps. The lawn had been recently cut, and the air was filled with the scent of just-mown grass.

Cal stopped the car about fifty yards from the house, even though there was room in the driveway right behind the fifteen-year-old Cadillac that had been polished to a glossy, almost-new finish. It was several minutes before he finally released his death grip on the steering wheel and turned off the engine.

"I guess she's home," he said, glancing at the huge black car.

"Do you want to see her alone?"

For just an instant, she caught the hint of panic in his eyes. "I think you have a right to be in on it."

"Not really."

"I want you there," he said gruffly, his tone partway between order and desperation.

Marilou reached over and squeezed his hand. "Cal, you're going to make an old woman very happy. Can that be so terrible?"

"If only it were that simple."

"It's only as complicated as you make it."

"Then it's damned complicated." He regarded the house warily before finally sighing heavily. "Come on, then. Let's go."

He clung to her hand as they crossed the yard. It was impossible to tell if he was holding on for moral support or simply because he feared she'd turn tail at the last minute and leave him alone to face his grandmother. His footsteps slowed as they neared the porch. At the steps, though, he squared his shoulders, gave her a smile that was sheer bravado and crossed the porch. When he rang the bell, they could hear the chimes sounding throughout the house.

It seemed to take forever before they heard any movement from within. The curtain over the leaded glass in the door was pushed aside, then fluttered back into place and the door swung open.

Marilou had expected some tiny, frail woman only barely able to leave her deathbed, but the woman who faced them was anything but tiny or frail. Stern-faced, her hair still thick and black and laced with threads of gray, she carried herself with incredible dignity. There was no way of telling from her expression what emotions were raging inside. Only her hand, curved around a carved, ivory-handled walking stick, gave away any hint of infirmity or distress. It trembled visibly as her gaze swept swiftly and indifferently over Marilou and settled avidly on her grandson.

"Cal," she said at once, without the slightest evidence of surprise or doubt. "You've come home."

Chapter Eleven

Cal faced the tall, reed-thin woman in the doorway and felt years of his life slide away. There was no doubt at all that this was his grandmother. From the almost coal-black hair and exotic features to the snapping blue eyes and imperious bearing, she looked exactly like his mother. For one lightning-swift instant, she'd appeared taken aback to find two strangers on her doorstep, but she recovered quickly.

When she spoke his name, he couldn't mistake the note of certainty and triumph in her voice. It was as if she'd been expecting him. The tension that had been coiled inside him wound tighter. Every finely honed instinct told him this had been a setup. She had stacked the deck, dealt the cards, then waited to come out a winner.

"Come in, boy," she ordered, still ignoring Marilou as if she were no more than a pesky nuisance. Her attitude annoyed the dickens out of him, but Marilou was apparently far too caught up in observing the by-play to be insulted.

"Don't just stand there," his grandmother badgered. "We're wasting heat."

Cal felt caught between furious indignation and admiration for her audacity. He wasn't sure exactly what sort of reception he'd expected, but this definitely wasn't it. He had been fooled by the frail handwriting and conciliatory tone, just as she'd expected him to be. Caroline Whitfield McDonald was obviously still very much in command, not only of all her faculties, but apparently—to her mind, anyway—of all she surveyed.

Something continued to puzzle him, though. How had she recognized him so readily? Had those detectives she'd hired sent her pictures? The possibility of such an invasion of his privacy unnerved him. Only a woman whose heart was made of steel would resort to such tactics. Now, as she stood aside, proud and dignified, waiting for them to enter, he remained rooted to the spot on the porch, leery of taking another step until he had some answers.

"What is it, boy?" she demanded.

"How did you know?" he said finally.

As his cool, curious gaze raked over her, a glimmer of a smile touched her thin lips. "There's nothing uncanny about it, boy. Come. I'll show you."

She ushered them into a parlor, where a fire blazed. She waved Marilou toward a chair. Then, after crossing to the grand piano that filled an incredibly large bay window, she picked up a silver-framed photograph and wordlessly handed it to him.

Cal's fingers trembled as he touched the cool metal frame. Aware of his grandmother and Marilou watching him expectantly, it took everything in him to actually look at the picture. When he did, he realized at once what she had seen in his face: his grandfather's features, the same dusky complexion, black hair and unexpectedly clear blue eyes. In the wedding picture in which his grandmother wore pristine satin and lace that flowed to the ground in luxurious folds, his grandfather looked uncomfortable in a tuxedo, the stern angles of his face softened as he stared lovingly at his beautiful bride.

Despite his wariness, Cal couldn't help smiling as he carefully placed the picture back among the dozens that were arranged haphazardly on the piano. "Yeah," he said thoughtfully, beginning to relax his guard ever so slightly. "I see what you mean."

"Look at the others, if you like."

He shook his head, deliberately not lingering on the snapshots and portraits of his mother. He couldn't help noticing, though, that there was no picture from his parents' wedding. Had they been forced to elope? How odd that he'd never known that, that he'd apparently never asked the questions most children did about how their parents met, about family ties and wedding albums.

"Sit, then," his grandmother insisted, grabbing a bell and ringing it as she settled herself in an antique rocker beside the fire. An old Mexican woman, her face a road map of wrinkles, appeared at once. Her sharp, brown-eyed gaze studied Cal and Marilou, and her face at once broke into a delighted smile.

"Por fin," she murmured fervently. "At last."

"Indeed," his grandmother said. Then, "Tea, Elena." She looked Marilou up and down. "And cake. She looks as though she could do with a little meat on her bones."

Marilou flushed, but remained silent, obviously intent on doing her part to make sure this reunion ran smoothly. His grandmother was staring hard at him. "You'd probably rather have a drink," she said, "but I don't keep the stuff, not after the way your grandfather drank himself into an early grave."

"I thought you said you'd driven him away."

"There's more than one way for a man to run. He hid in a bottle. Maybe he figured that way he'd make life hell for both of us."

Though regret flashed briefly in her eyes, her tone was all self-righteous indignation and harsh judgment. He wondered fleetingly if she'd always been this hard, this uncompromising.

"Tea will be fine," he said at last, unable to take his eyes off the woman who reminded him so much of his mother. Unwanted memories were flooding back, along with all of the pain. Right this instant he resented the hell out of Marilou for having forced him to come, and he hated his grandmother and all she stood for.

"What're you staring at, boy?" she demanded, when Elena had retreated. "Were you expecting to find me with one foot in my grave?"

"Your letter did say you were dying," he retorted calmly, unwilling to admit the direction in which his thoughts had actually strayed.

"We all do."

Instantly suspicious, he felt Marilou stiffen beside him as well. "But you're not ill?" he said, his glance toward Marilou meant to convey I-told-you-so.

His grandmother thumped her cane impatiently. "Of course I'm ill. I'm eighty years old. I'm tired. I can't keep up with things the way I used to. My bones ache from autumn right through spring. The doctor says my heart's failing. The old fool. What else would it be doing at my age?" Her gaze narrowed. "Is that why you're here? Did you come to pay your last respects? Don't expect to dance on my grave too soon."

Cal realized then that despite his natural caution, he had been touched by Marilou's eternal optimism. In some secret part of himself he had dared to harbor one scant hope for a real relationship. It withered irrevocably under her cutting tone and the admission that she'd deliberately tricked him into coming. Stunned to discover how much it hurt, he got to his feet and grabbed his coat. "We're out of here. This was a mistake. Come on, Marilou."

"No," she said softly, her gaze fastened on his grandmother.

He stood where he was and regarded her incredulously. "What is wrong with you? You can see for yourself that the letter was some damned ruse to drag me here. This isn't *Little House on the Prairie,* dammit. Not every family melodrama has a happy ending. Can't you see that yet?"

He glowered at his grandmother, who sat rigidly, listening to his tirade with no hint of emotion. Her apparent indifference kept him going. "She's just a scheming old woman who's used to getting her way, and we've played straight into her hands."

Marilou shook her head. "That's not the way it is, is it?" she said pointedly to his grandmother.

"I don't know what you're talking about, girl," the old woman said, but her shoulders suddenly weren't quite as stiff as they had been, and her tone lacked starch. Cal saw that her gnarled hands were knotted together tensely in her lap.

Marilou shook her head impatiently. "You two! I have never met two people more obviously cut from the same cloth. You're both stubborn as mules. Can't either one of you just admit that you need each other?"

"What makes you think that?" his grandmother demanded. "I've gotten along for all these years..."

"So have I," Cal insisted.

"Terrific," Marilou said, obviously beginning to warm up to the fight. Her words dripped sarcasm. "You've gotten along. Is that enough?" She turned to his grandmother. "If so, why did you write that letter?"

"I needed to get some things off my chest. That's all."

"You wanted him to come," Marilou contradicted.

"No, she *expected* me to come," Cal muttered in disgust. "There's a difference."

"I've learned not to expect anything," his grandmother retorted, glaring at him. "Not from family."

"Ditto." Cal scowled right back at her.

"Oh, for heaven's sake," Marilou said. "I am going into the kitchen to help Elena with the tea. When I come back, I expect you two to be behaving like civilized adults instead of a couple of spoiled brats."

When she'd stalked out of the room, Cal felt suddenly bereft. Though she seemed to take some perverse pleasure in needling him, Marilou had at least served as a buffer. Now he was left with his grandmother all alone. He would have preferred facing something easy, like a firing squad.

She simply sat there waiting, dressed all in black as if she were all ready for a funeral. He wondered how many years she'd worn the drab mourning outfits. Had it begun when his grandfather died? Had she settled permanently into the role of bereaved widow out of some sense of guilt, guilt which had only been compounded when his mother ran off? He was still trying to figure out what made her tick, when he realized she'd spoken.

"What?"

"She's an outspoken little thing, isn't she?" his grandmother said with grudging admiration. "Where'd you find her?"

"Actually she found me. Your letter went astray. She saw that I got it."

"I suppose I ought to thank her, then."

"Frankly I'd prefer to strangle her."

"You sleeping with her?"

He flushed angrily and began to pace. "That's none of your business, old woman."

"It is if you're going to be staying under my roof. There is certain behavior I don't tolerate. I don't care how old-fashioned that makes me."

"Who the hell said anything about staying here?"

"Well, where else would you stay?"

"We have a room in Cheyenne."

"That's too far away."

"So, you're actually admitting that you wanted me here," he said, managing a wry grin.

She waved a bejeweled hand dismissively. "Oh, for pity's sake, of course I did."

"Then why couldn't you just say that?"

"For the same reason you didn't want to come, I expect. For all that we're family, we don't know each other. I find it difficult enough to trust folks I do know."

"Same here," he admitted reluctantly.

Piercing eyes regarded him intently. "You planning on sticking around long enough for us to get to know each other?"

"I don't know," he said honestly. "Everything in me tells me to take off."

"Whitfields are not cowards."

"My name is Rivers, grandmother. Have you conveniently forgotten my father?"

"You're still a Whitfield, through and through. You might move on a bit too readily, but you've got gumption that your daddy never had."

"How the hell would you know that? You said in your letter you ran him off before you ever had a chance to know him."

"He chose to go, and he talked your mother into running with him. A real man would have stayed right here and proved me wrong."

"A real man would never have let you dominate him, and I doubt you'd have tolerated that for very long. You're a bully, Grandmother. I've known you less than an hour and I can see that."

"Because you know all about bullying and getting your own way. I'd say we're evenly matched. You have to admit that makes the prospect of sticking around into an almost irresistible challenge for a man like you."

Cal suddenly caught the glint of amusement in her eyes and found yet more of the tension sliding away. He chuckled. "I do like a challenge," he admitted.

His grandmother nodded toward the kitchen. "That one's a challenge, too, isn't she?"

"You could say that," he admitted ruefully.

It would have been wrong to describe the sound she made as flat-out laughter, but it was probably the closest the sour old thing had come in years. "Then I'd say you have your hands full, boy. You can't let a couple of women get the best of you now, can you?"

He laughed at that. "No, I don't suppose I can."

"Good. You'll take the room at the end of the hall. She can have the one next to me."

"Then you'd damn well better be a heavy sleeper," he taunted.

"We'll just see about that. Now go on in the kitchen and drink your tea, then go get your things. I'll see you at dinner." She struggled to her feet. "I think I'd better have a nap now."

For the first time he detected a slight unsteadiness before she determinedly straightened her back and marched off, leaving him to ponder how she'd managed to shanghai him into doing exactly what she'd wanted him to do. He wondered how Marilou was going to react to the news that they were moving in.

Why wonder, he thought disgustedly, he knew exactly how she was going to react. Even as furious as she was with him, he could have staked money that she'd be thrilled by this outcome. When it came to family, she was entirely predictable.

"Why aren't you in there with your grandmother?" she demanded when he ventured into the cozy kitchen that was filled with the scent of apple pie and cinnamon. She and Elena were sitting at the table contentedly sipping tea and eating thick, fudgy brownies.

"I can see that you were in a real rush to get back to us," he observed, pouring himself a cup of tea and grabbing one of the brownies.

"The *señorita* and I, we agree you need time to get reacquainted," Elena said.

"Believe me, we already know everything we need to know about each other," he said. "She's an aggressive, manipulative, calculating woman."

Marilou shook her head. "Interesting how you choose to use those words to denigrate her, when you'd find them essential in a business opponent."

"I came here looking for a grandmother, not a tycoon."

"Sounds sexist to me," Marilou said.

"Okay, okay, we're all agreed that this is going to be a fair fight among equals. Notice," he said, dropping an impulsive kiss on her cheek, "that I included you among the combatants."

"Not me. I'm just an innocent bystander."

"Not anymore. If I'm moving in here, you're coming along, which puts you smack in the middle of the fray."

Marilou nearly choked at that. "We're moving here?"

"Under this very roof, though with a very discreet distance from your bedroom to mine."

He watched for some sign of disappointment but she simply stilled, and that flash of pain he'd put in her eyes last night returned to haunt him. He glanced sideways at Elena, who had busied herself at the stove, then finally shrugged. This was not the time to have a discussion about last night.

"I think maybe this is a bad idea," Marilou said finally.

He stared at her. "What are you talking about? I thought this was exactly what you wanted."

"For you and your grandmother, yes. I don't belong here now. I should go back to Atlanta."

"Absolutely not," he said, immediately resorting to blackmail to get her to stay. "If you go, I go."

"Cal," she protested.

"No. That's it. We stay together or we go together. I'm only doing this for you."

"Dammit, Cal, I don't want you to do this for me. This is your life, your family."

"Right now, you are a part of that life."

"Right now," she repeated wistfully, staring determinedly into her cup. He wondered if she was aware of the salty tears that splashed into the tea.

Damn, why couldn't he give her more than that? She was a woman who deserved happily-ever-afters, if anyone did. He should let her go so that she could find them. Instead, though, he knew that he'd never make it through the next couple of days without her there to badger him on.

"Please stay," he said finally.

She gazed up at him then, her expression as close to helpless as he was ever likely to see it. It wrenched his heart to see her torn in two like that and to know that he was responsible. "I'll stay," she said finally.

In that instant Cal realized that he was, in fact, every bit as manipulative as his grandmother. Of all the damned things to inherit.

Chapter Twelve

Settling into the McDonald ranch life was a mixed blessing for Marilou. Though she loved watching the nonstop sparring between Cal and his grandmother, for the most part she had absolutely nothing to do. Though Cal invited her along when he toured the place with the old woman, Marilou always made her excuses and declined. She was determined that the two of them get to know each other without her around as the buffer Cal intended her to be. She offered to help Elena, but the energetic housekeeper flatly refused.

"You are a houseguest, *señorita*. It would not be right," Elena said. "There are books in the library, if you wish to read. Or you could ride. One of the men would be glad to saddle a horse for you."

"Maybe I'll just go for a walk," she said finally, grabbing a bright red jacket to ward off the bone-chilling wind that felt very little like spring.

Despite the brisk breeze, the sky was clear, and wildflowers were beginning to bloom. In no time at all, her lonely, depressed mood began to lift. After more than an hour of wandering, she came to an old tree that had apparently been toppled by lightning and never cleared. Drawing her jacket more snugly around her, she climbed onto the weathered tree trunk and stared at the sparse, magnificent scenery, thinking about how much had happened to her in the month since she had made the impulsive decision to go after Cal.

She'd been to places she'd only dreamed about, experienced things she'd only read about and, most amazing of all, she had fallen deeply, irrevocably, head over heels in love. Unfortunately the man happened to be a pigheaded idiot who was clinging to his self-imposed emotional isolation with the tenacity of a pit bull. Sooner or later she was going to have to accept the fact that while Cal might come to love her, he might very well never trust her... or any woman, for that matter.

As if she'd conjured him, he suddenly slid his arms around her waist from behind. He smelled of wood smoke and fresh air with the faintest hint of the after-shave he'd used hours earlier. He nuzzled the back of her neck, sending warmth catapulting through her.

"You look far too serious for such a beautiful day," he accused gently. "What were you thinking about?"

"Oh, cabbages and kings."

"Hmm, must have been me."

She turned and grinned at him, rubbing her hand against his cheek. "Which are you, a cabbage or a king?"

"That's probably a matter of opinion. Want to come for a ride with me? It'll dust the cobwebs from your mind."

She shook her head.

"How come?"

"I don't ride," she admitted reluctantly.

Cal stared at her, clearly astonished. "But you spent all that time around the horses in Florida."

"Around them, not on them. Do you think Chaney was about to let me on one of your precious Thoroughbreds?"

"We have stable ponies, too. All you had to do was ask."

"I guess the right time just never presented itself."

He reached for her hand. "Then that's about to change. Let's go, sweetheart."

"Cal," she protested weakly, though her pulse had already kicked in with excitement at the prospect of one more adventure. Life with Cal would always . . .

Life with Cal couldn't be, she reminded herself sternly. There was only now, these next few days, and the adventure would be over for her. Maybe, though, when she got home and she would get out her camera equipment again. Maybe she would try to pick up where she had left off. The prospect gave her something to look forward to besides the loneliness.

"Let's go," she said, jumping to the ground. "I'll race you back to the barn."

She took off at a run, knowing she would be beat, laughing anyway at the sheer exhilaration of the race, delighted when Cal passed her, then turned and caught her in an exuberant embrace. His lips on hers were cold as ice, but they held the power of fire. His hands slid inside her jacket and found her breasts, the nipples already tightened into hard buds from the brisk air and already sensitive in anticipation of his touch.

"Have you forgiven me?" he said, his eyes riveted to hers.

"For what?"

"For hurting you the other night?"

"You were honest with me, Cal. It's always better to know the truth, even if you don't like it."

"I wish..."

Her heart in her throat and tears threatening, she pressed a finger against his lips. "Shh. No matter what happens, I will always remember this time in my life. You've made these weeks special for me."

"You are an incredible woman, Marilou Stockton."

She wasn't sure she could bear to hear another word. "And you are a man who promised to teach me to ride. Are you welshing on that promise?"

"Never."

"Then show me how to get on one of these beasts. Who knows, maybe I'll decide I want to become a jockey."

"Sweetheart, as much as I adore your cute little figure, as perfect as I think you are, you are about five inches too tall and ten pounds too heavy to be a jockey."

She frowned. "That is a problem. I could probably lose the weight, but there's not much I can do about the height. I guess I'll just have to settle for riding the range or something."

"First, let's just see how you do riding around this paddock."

"Is that a note of skepticism I hear?"

He laughed. "You won't catch me with that. No comment."

"Wise man."

Though it would have taken torture to pry the admission out of her, Marilou had to concede that Cal had been fairly close to the mark in analyzing her skill. She hurt in places that no lady ever discussed. For once, since the visit to Mrs. McDonald began, she was very glad that she and Cal had been banished to separate bedrooms. She would have hated like crazy to moan with pain the minute he tried to touch her. Not that he remained entirely aloof, but fortunately her lips seemed to be one of the few places not battered and bruised by this latest adventure. And Cal was a very inventive kisser.

The days took on an easy rhythm. The three of them had breakfast together, then Cal and his grandmother huddled together to discuss the ranch. Occasionally Marilou sat in on the conversations, liking them best when they veered into family history. Though listening at times emphasized her place as an outsider, she was still delighted that Cal was slowly beginning to acknowledge his place as a McDonald heir.

"Your books are a shambles," he announced late one morning, rubbing his temples after hours of staring at page after page of figures written in his grandmother's cramped handwriting. Marilou had long since given up trying to decipher it and sat sipping yet another cup of English breakfast tea. She was becoming addicted to the stuff. Cal's grandmother provided a different variety of tea for practically every hour of the day.

"You need to get a computer," Cal said, not for the first time. To Marilou it was beginning to be like background music. Her thoughts wandered, then refocused as he added, "Or at the very least an accountant."

"I'm too old to learn all that technical nonsense," his grandmother insisted predictably, glowering at him. "And if I've learned one thing about money, it's that no one will watch over it as well as you do it yourself."

"If that isn't the most old-fashioned, set-in-your-ways thinking I've ever heard," he grumbled. "I could never run a business, if I didn't share some of the responsibilities."

"I have men to run the cattle," his grandmother offered.

"I'm surprised," he retorted.

Marilou chuckled. She'd been listening to Cal and his grandmother bickering like this since breakfast. They'd had the exact same argument the past three mornings. As far as she was concerned, it was heavenly. Only strangers maintained a polite facade. Families fought and nagged and loved in equal measures. Apparently Elena agreed. She'd stopped hovering over Mrs. McDonald and now bustled around with an approving smile on her face, content that the uproar in the house was a happy one.

"Why should I hire an accountant when I have you to figure it out for me?" his grandmother finally said slyly.

Cal threw down his pencil. "Because I won't be around."

"Hmph!"

"Grandmother, I have told you repeatedly that I have to go back to Florida by the beginning of the week. I have my own business to run and I've been away too long already."

"Race horses," she said with a derisive sniff. "Cattle, that's the thing. Been good enough for the Whitfields for all these generations. Don't see why it's not good enough for you."

"I'm only one-quarter Whitfield."

"Must be the stubborn quarter," Marilou offered.

Two pairs of blue eyes glowered at her. She grinned happily. "I don't suppose I could talk the two of you into going for a drive instead of sitting around sniping at each other. It's a lovely day. The air is balmy at last. Elena said she'd pack us a picnic—fried chicken, deviled eggs, the works."

A spark of longing flared in Mrs. McDonald's eyes, then she shook her head. "The ground's too cold for these old bones, but you two run along."

"We'll take a blanket," Marilou promised. "You'll be fine."

A smile played about the old lady's lips, and for an instant she seemed lost in reminiscence. "It would be pleasant, I suppose. Your grandfather and I . . ." She sighed. "Well, that was a long time ago."

"Please come," Marilou begged. "You can tell us more about the family."

She knew that was a surefire lure. Mrs. McDonald had been using every opportunity to seduce Cal with those fascinating tales of his ancestors, men who'd pioneered in the West, surviving droughts and natural disasters, forging what had become something of a cattle empire. Apparently she hoped to convince him that he would be abandoning his heritage if he didn't stay and claim the ranch as his own. Periodically Marilou had dared to add her own subtle hints along the same lines.

"If you two are planning to gang up on me again, I'll pass and stay here," he said now, but Marilou caught the tolerant amusement in his eyes. He was beginning to care for the old woman. She could hear the tenderness in his voice more and more frequently.

"You aren't afraid of a couple of women, are you?" she inquired innocently.

"Damned right I am. When it comes to the two of you, any man would be a fool if he didn't watch his backside all the time. Last night some crumbling old diary turned up under my pillow. I don't suppose either of you knows how it got there."

"Not me," Marilou said cheerfully. "I've been banned from that end of the hall."

"And you?" he inquired, directing his gaze at his grandmother.

"I might have mentioned something to Elena . . ."

"Lord, you mean she's in on it, too? I haven't got a prayer."

"I like a man who recognizes a worthy opponent," Mrs. McDonald said approvingly. "Now stop dilly-dallying, boy. If we're going, let's go. Elena will be furious if we ruin her lunch."

As soon as they were all in the car, Cal turned to Marilou. "I suppose you know exactly where you want to go."

She grinned. "Well, your grandmother did mention that there was a creek along the eastern edge of the property."

He sighed. "How far?"

Marilou exchanged a conspiratorial glance with Mrs. McDonald. "Not far," they said in unison.

It took a little over an hour to get there. Cal was muttering under his breath by the time they finally came to the creek that wound its way through the distant pastures. Even he had to admit, though, that the setting was spectacular. Wildflowers had painted the spring landscape in shades of purple, yellow and red.

Sunlight glinted off the shallow creek bed. Cattle roamed in the distance. And on the far edge of the horizon were the faint purple shadows of the mountains.

From the back seat of the car, Marilou heard Mrs. McDonald sigh. "It's every bit as beautiful this time of year as I remember," she said.

Cal turned to study her, a worried frown on his brow. "How long has it been since you were out here?"

"A while," she evaded.

"Grandmother?"

"Last spring."

"Why so long?"

Marilou already knew the answer to that. Elena had confided that over the past year Mrs. McDonald had found it increasingly difficult to get around. The doctors blamed it on osteoporosis and arthritis. There were days, the housekeeper lamented, when the old woman wasn't able to get out of bed at all. Even now she was in far more pain than she'd been letting on to the two of them, but she'd apparently been determined that Cal would never see it. Marilou felt it wasn't her secret to share, but she hoped that soon Mrs. McDonald would tell Cal the whole truth about her rapidly deteriorating condition. She also knew that the old woman didn't want him staying on out of pity.

Even now she didn't so much as hint at the truth. She merely said, "I was busy. Besides, I pay that lazy manager to see to things for me."

"If you don't trust your books to anyone, how can you entrust responsibility for the rest to someone you've repeatedly described to me as lazy and inept?"

"What choice do I have? I can't ride a horse anymore. The men don't take orders well from an old lady. Even Garrett's got more command over them than I would."

"Maybe I should have a talk with him."

Mrs. McDonald smiled contentedly. "Yes, dear, why don't you do that? I expect Garrett back any day now."

"If you think this Garrett's reliable, maybe you should try giving him more authority. I suspect he's chafing at the bit to really take charge of this place."

"That chance will come along soon enough. When I can't draw breath enough to make a few decisions, I'll just lay down and die. Then, since you keep insisting that you will be nothing more than an absentee landlord, Garrett can take over."

Marilou caught Cal's agitation. He was practically grinding his teeth. "Grandmother, how many times do I have to tell you that I do not want you to leave this place to me?"

She waved off his comment, as she had each of the other times. "And just who should I leave it to, if not to family?"

He didn't answer right away. Finally he suggested quietly, "You could leave it to Mother."

"She turned her back on it."

"You sent her away."

"She could have come back."

"Hat in hand, I suppose?"

"Don't be ridiculous. I never wanted her to beg. It would have been better for everyone if I'd been wrong about the marriage. I wasn't."

"You told me you're sorry. Why can't you tell her?"

"I told her. She didn't want to hear it."

"That was years ago. Try again."

Marilou was startled by Cal's vehemence. He'd made a lot of strides in his relationship with his grandmother, but she hadn't expected him to suddenly take his mother's side this way. Maybe everything was going to fall into place just the way she'd imagined it. Sitting out here in the warm spring air, the sun bright in the clearest blue sky she'd ever seen, it was possible once again to believe in miracles and happy endings.

"Maybe you could call her," she suggested hesitantly. The last time she'd suggested he work for a reconciliation between his mother and grandmother, he'd bitten her head off. Today he seemed mellow enough to listen.

"It's not my fight," he said, staring pointedly at his grandmother.

"That doesn't mean..."

Mrs. McDonald touched Marilou's hand. "No, girl, he's right. This is something I should do...if anyone does it."

"Will you, then?" Marilou asked with surprising urgency. In her heart she knew that this was the final step if any real healing was ever to take place.

Mrs. McDonald stared at her. "My dear, why does this matter so much to you?"

She shrugged. "I know it's none of my business."

"That isn't what I said. Why do you feel so strongly about it?"

"I just think families ought to stick together. You've been talking about family history ever since we got here. Don't you have some responsibility to see that the tradition goes on?" she challenged.

The old woman's gaze faltered at that. Then she sighed. "I'll give it some thought. Now why don't you two go take a walk together? I'm sure you'd like some time alone."

Cal's eyes met Marilou's and he winked.

"How do you know we haven't been sneaking off to be together at night?"

"Because the floorboards in that hall creak under a mouse's step. You two have been staying put, just like I told you to."

"That's no way to get great-grandchildren," Cal challenged, sending Marilou's pulse caroming wildly.

His grandmother waved her cane at him. "There will be no illegitimate great-grandbabies in this family. Not if I have anything to say about it. You make an honest woman of this girl and I'll build you a whole private suite."

Marilou's breath caught in her throat as she watched for Cal's reaction. His expression sobered at once, all too quickly it seemed to her. Suddenly she wanted to run, to feel the warm breeze against her cheeks, the grass against her bare feet. She wanted to get away from Cal and his insensitive teasing, and from all the things that could never be.

Cal was already standing over her, though, his hand extended. "Come on. It seems we're not needed around here."

Marilou was slow to get up, unwilling to be lured into Cal's spell so easily. Stalling for time, she turned to Mrs. McDonald worriedly. "What will you do?"

"I'll do some thinking, maybe a little remembering. I'll be just fine. Run along and enjoy yourselves."

They were barely out of sight before Cal slid his arms around Marilou's waist and pulled her tight against him. His lips met hers, lightly at first, then with more demand. She tried to hold back, tried not to let his warmth flood through her, his mouth persuade her, but it was useless. She would have forever to miss being in his arms. She wouldn't give up the spine-tingling sensations—couldn't give them up—before she had to.

Chapter Thirteen

Keeping his defenses securely in place was getting to be increasingly difficult for Cal. As a hardheaded businessman himself, his admiration for his grandmother's gritty determination and amazing spirit grew day by day, though he wasn't about to tell her that. She was too damned sure of herself as it was. Admittedly, though, the thriving ranch was a testament to her intelligence and feistiness. It couldn't have been easy for a woman in her position to take on such a vast empire back during the Depression and keep it going during decades when others had been turning their property over to oil exploration or sheep ranching.

"Once a cattleman, always a cattleman," she said staunchly when he asked how she had withstood the pressures to change.

"Sometimes being a stubborn, willful woman has served you well," he noted wryly.

"It has always served me well," she corrected with a smile.

"You really must do something about those books, though. And I'd like to see you diversifying your investments. Why don't I bring Joshua out for a few days to help you out?"

His grandmother regarded him suspiciously. "Who is this Joshua person?"

"My accountant and my friend. I've known him almost all my life. He's the most trustworthy, honorable man I know. I'll have him fly out tomorrow, in fact," he said decisively. Once he knew his grandmother's finances were under control, he'd feel free to go back to Florida. This was definitely the best course of action, he thought, though Marilou was staring at him, her expression horrified.

"What's wrong?" he demanded, though he suspected he knew.

"Don't you think you ought to speak with Joshua first, before making that kind of commitment for him?"

That was the last thing he'd been expecting. He'd anticipated another lecture on running away. "Why?"

"Cal, you've said it yourself. He hates isolation. This place would make him crazy. Isn't there someone else you could hire?"

"I'm not asking him to move here, just to spend a couple of days."

"He'll consider it a lifetime. He got nervous the minute he set foot outside his car that day he drove over to Ocala."

Somehow he found it irritating that Marilou had zeroed in so readily on Joshua's idiosyncrasies and now felt compelled to jump to his defense.

"He'll survive," he grumbled. "In fact, the change will do him good. He's too stuffy for his own good. He could use a little adventure in his life."

"Garrett might make it a little more palatable for him," his grandmother said slyly.

Cal and Marilou whirled on her. "What?" they said in unison.

"She's a real beauty, though there's not a sign that she's aware of it."

"Garrett is a woman?" Cal said incredulously.

His grandmother stared at him with masterful innocence. "Of course, she is."

"*Of course?* You never said."

"You never asked."

"That seems to be a problem of his," Marilou piped in cheerfully. Cal glared at her.

"Why does it bother you so much that my foreman is a woman?"

"It doesn't bother me. It just surprises me."

"And you don't like surprises," Marilou inserted. "Any more than Joshua would. You can't drag him into this without warning him, Cal."

"About what, Garrett?"

"Oh, stop being impossible. I suspect Joshua knows how to handle most women."

"I repeat," his grandmother said, "he hasn't met Garrett."

"Did someone mention my name?" a slender blonde asked from the doorway.

Marilou was gaping. With her long legs and tiny waist, Garrett belonged on the cover of a magazine, something definitely more upscale than a farm journal. Her hair fell nearly to her hips, her features were fragile, but there was a lean athleticism about her that no doubt came from years of handling heavy chores. Men's chores.

"You're Garrett?" Cal said, knowing Marilou was watching Garrett speculatively, clearly sizing her up with her finely honed woman's intuition. From the grin that was slowly spreading across Marilou's face, he forgot all about jealousy and decided that Joshua's bachelor days were seriously numbered. He noticed that she didn't voice another objection to calling his friend.

"I'm surprised," he said finally, grasping the hand that was held out to him.

Garrett turned a chiding gaze on his grandmother. "She loves to do that to people. My real name is Tracy Garrett. If I hadn't gotten hooked on using my last name years ago, she wouldn't be able to get away with it. Sorry I was away when you arrived. Mrs. Mac sent me over to Montana to take a look at some stock."

"What did you think?" his grandmother asked, suddenly all business. "Did you spend a bundle of my money?"

"I left you pocket change," Garrett retorted, then gave a concise but obviously knowledgeable report, including the amount she'd spent for the cattle. He listened closely, impressed not only with her acumen, but with the way his grandmother deferred to her judgment. She didn't bat an eye at a dollar figure that had Marilou gasping and even left him a little startled. Apparently even at eighty there was nothing conservative about his grandmother's approach to business.

Dinner turned into a lively affair. Garrett had a knack for keeping everyone off guard with her insightful comments and wry wit. There was absolutely no pretense about her, not in the way she dressed or the straightforward way she talked. And Casey, her twelve-year-old daughter, was a real hellion. She and his grandmother had a rapport that made Cal oddly envious.

He felt ridiculous being jealous of a precocious child, but he couldn't help wondering how much different his life might have been if he'd grown up around here, instead of turning up years later as an interloper. He was feeling easier here by the day, more at home. Not that he intended for one second to stay, but at least he wasn't on pins and needles with the anxious need to run. He was glad, after all, that he'd had this chance to meet the old woman, and he owed Marilou for that.

He glanced across the table and saw that she was thoroughly engrossed in the lively conversation between his grandmother and Garrett. One of the things he loved the most about Marilou was the way she fit in without needing to be the center of attention. Few women could do that happily, but she seemed to thrive on staying in the background and seeing that everyone else had a wonderful time. It was a knack that he was increasingly coming to treasure.

She looked up just then, caught him watching her and smiled. Her green eyes shimmered in the candlelight in a way that made his heart skid wildly. Suddenly he needed her, wanted her more than he'd ever wanted another woman. Regret over the distance they'd been forced to keep between them the past few days slammed into him.

He leaned closer. "Feel like a walk?" he whispered under his breath, reaching for her hand beneath the table. He captured it in her lap, watching with delight as fire crept into her cheeks.

"Shouldn't we stay?" she said, her rapt gaze never leaving his face.

He glanced toward his grandmother, who nodded subtly. "Oh, I think we'd be forgiven," he said.

"Can I come?" Garrett's daughter chimed in, already partway out of her chair, confident of her welcome.

Cal had barely restrained a groan, when Garrett said, "No, you may not. It's almost your bedtime and you have studying to do."

"School's almost out. What's the point?" she grumbled, casting an appealing glance around the table. Help was not forthcoming.

"The point is that I expect you to do as you're told, young lady."

Casey grinned at Mrs. McDonald. "What's that word you told me the other day?"

"Martinet," she said, her lips twitching. Cal chuckled at the obvious conspiracy between the two of them.

"Yeah, mom. That's what you are, an old martinet."

"I may be a rigid disciplinarian, but I am hardly old," Garrett responded, her eyes flashing. "If you doubt that, I'll race you to our cottage. The loser will do dishes for the entire summer."

"You're on," Casey said, scrambling up with a whoop. Her mother rolled her eyes at Cal's grandmother. "Sorry, Mrs. Mac. She was locked up in the car too long today."

"Seems to me that might be true for both of you," Mrs. McDonald said. "Run along, dear. We'll talk more in the morning."

She peered at Cal when they'd gone. "I thought you were going for a walk."

"In a minute," he said, settling back into his place at the table. He still had a firm grip on Marilou's hand, which she kept trying without success to move to less volatile territory. "Why on earth did you tell me that your manager was lazy and inept? It's obvious to me that Garrett is neither and that you wouldn't tolerate it if she were."

"Yes, well . . ." Her voice trailed off guiltily.

"Come on, grandmother," he prodded. "What's the real story?"

"You can't blame an old woman for trying."

"Trying what?" he asked, completely bemused. Then in a flash it came to him. "Of course. You figured if I felt the whole business was about to come apart, I'd stick around to help save it."

"Okay, yes," she confessed without flinching. "It occurred to me, if it was something you could get your teeth into, you'd see the need for staying."

"And the books? Did you prepare that awful set just for me?"

His grandmother smiled faintly. "No. I guarantee that they are every bit the shambles you found them to be. Garrett has no more interest in bookkeeping than I do."

"Does that mean you won't object to my bringing Joshua out here?"

"Seems to me, from what Marilou has said, that Joshua's the one most likely to object."

"Don't worry about that. I pay him well enough to justify some occasional discomfort on his part."

"Then bring him on. I'm fresh out of ammunition to keep you around."

He was just about to leave the table and take that much-delayed walk, when he heard the note of resignation in her voice. It wavered pitifully. She could have been faking it, but he couldn't bring himself to risk it. "Grandmother, this doesn't mean I'll never come back."

She sighed heavily. "We'll see."

"I promise."

Despite his promise, though, he couldn't shake the image of the way she looked as they left the dining room, her shoulders slumped and her face etched with sadness.

"So, what did you think of Garrett?" Marilou asked, when she and Cal were outside. Stars were scattered across the sky by the zillions, tiny sparks of fairy dust that enchanted her. She shivered in the cool night air, and Cal draped his jacket around her.

"I think hiring her was probably the smartest thing my grandmother ever did. They seem to get along well, don't you think?"

"I suppose."

Cal paused, and she sensed his sudden confusion over her disinterested tone. He touched two fingers to her chin and tilted it up until their eyes met. "Why the lack of enthusiasm? I thought you liked her."

"I do. I really do. It's just that she's not . . ."

"She's not family," Cal completed wearily. "Marilou, I can't stay here. I don't want to stay here. Getting to know my grandmother has changed my life in a lot of ways. There's a lot to be said for knowing that you have solid roots somewhere, but she and I are too much alike to ever live peacefully in the same county, much less the same house. If that's what you were hoping for, I'm sorry."

She sighed. "Deep down I know you're right. But the past couple of days here, I've felt something I'd really missed."

"That sense of belonging," he said, surprising her with his understanding. "I know. I've seen it on your face. You do fit in, every bit as much as I do."

She shook her head. "No. When you get right down to it, even though your grandmother and Elena have been wonderful, I'm still an outsider. I always will be."

"You'll always be welcome here. You know that."

"I suppose," she agreed.

She heard the catch in Cal's breath, felt the uneasy silence that fell between them and cursed herself for spoiling such a lovely, romantic spring evening. Still, if a clock had ticked loudly and symbolically in the background, she would have been no more aware that their time together was slipping away.

It hurt. And if Cal didn't kiss her very soon and very hard, she was going to start bawling like a baby, and that would really mess things up. She wanted to leave with a brave front so that he would always remember her as a tough lady. If there was one thing she knew that Cal Rivers respected, it was a woman with grit.

Since she needed his arms around her more than she feared rejection, she turned and slid hers around his waist. "Hold me," she said softly. "Please."

When she was crushed against him, when she could hear the steady rhythm of his heart, when she could feel the tensing of his muscles and his heat under her fingertips, she finally felt safe. He stood there rocking with her for the longest time, before both hands slid up to frame her face.

"What's this?" he murmured, brushing away tears with the pad of his thumbs. "Why so sad?"

"I don't know," she denied.

"Liar. Come on. Don't you know you can tell me anything?"

She nodded. "I'm just being silly."

"About what?"

"I just realized that I'll never get to see Dawn's Magic on the track or get to muck out the stalls or see how my tomatoes turned out." She forced a wobbly grin. "That is if I even left any tomato plants in the ground when I weeded."

Cal seemed taken aback by what she said, or maybe by the desolation in her tone. Then he got this far-away look in his eyes. "I never really thought that far ahead," he said finally, his voice flat.

"It's okay," she said at once, drawing on sheer bravado. "I mean this is the way things were supposed to turn out. I did my job. You're back with your grandmother. I should be happy."

"Then why does it feel like we're getting ready to go to a funeral around here," he said, humor teasing at his lips but not quite tilting the corners into a smile.

"Beats me," she said jauntily. "I can't explain it."

His arms tightened around her. He drew in a deep breath, then said firmly, "Well, I can. We're both behaving like a couple of idiots when there's an obvious solution here."

"I sure don't see one."

"Of course there is. You'll just come back to Florida with me."

Marilou's pulse kicked in like a filly's at the sight of a racetrack.

"I mean, it makes perfect sense," he went on, his enthusiasm clearly mounting. "You want to be there. Chaney's missing your blueberry muffins. I . . . I care for you. Why not, Marilou? You're not all that anxious to go back to your old job. Pack up your things and move down to live with us. I promise you that you'd never regret it."

After her first initial, dazed reaction, Marilou actually listened to Cal's words. Maybe if he hadn't stumbled over that one hurried phrase summing up his feelings, she could have bought the act. Instead his pretty speech simply didn't add up to a proposal, no matter how desperately she tried to shape it into one.

"What exactly are you offering?" she said finally, taking a step away so she could see his face more clearly.

"A place to live, a job." He appeared to hesitate for an instant before adding cautiously, "Me, if you'll have me."

"You?"

He frowned. "Look, I know it's not exactly conventional, but we'd be good together. You know that. These past few weeks are the happiest I've ever had. We don't fight. Well, not much anyway."

"What about love?" she said grimly. "What about those great-grandbabies you were talking to your grandmother about?"

He looked as if she'd leveled a two-by-four straight at his stomach. This time he was the one stepping back, so quickly that it made her heart ache.

"You know that's not possible," he said, his voice low and tight, maybe with anger, maybe with pain.

"Why isn't it possible?" she said, deliberately provoking him into an argument. She was spoiling for a fight now, a really good one. Maybe it would help her to forget about how much it hurt. "Are you telling me I'm good enough to live with, attractive enough to sleep with, but not special enough to marry?"

"This has nothing to do with you."

"How can you say that?"

"Because *I'm* the problem. I'll never marry. You've known that from the first."

"But I have never understood why. I'm not even sure you do. Your words are an automatic response. It's as if you've told that to yourself for so many years now that you've convinced yourself it's the way your life has to be."

"I told myself that, because it was the truth. I'm sorry I can't give you what you'd hoped for, but you'd never regret being with me, Marilou. You'd have everything you ever dreamed of, including the freedom to leave anytime you wanted to. I'd never hold you."

"Do you honestly expect that to please me?" She stared at him in amazement. "You do, don't you? Cal, I'll admit that love is giving someone the freedom to go or stay, but it's also trust and commitment. It's sharing the good times and the bad, not running off whenever it's convenient or whenever things get a little sticky. You can't build a relationship on any less, whether there's a marriage license attached to it or not.''

He heard her out, his hands stuffed in his pockets, his shoulders squared. ''Since I can't offer what you want, I guess you'll be going then.''

She wondered if he even heard the raw anguish in his voice. ''I don't see that I have any choice. I can't be happy with the terms you're offering.'' She dared one last touch, her fingers lingering on his cheek. ''The hell of it is, I don't think you can be, either.''

As soon as the words were out of her mouth, she turned and walked away. She wanted to run, as far and as fast as she could, but she wouldn't, not with him watching.

Marilou spent the endless night packing and pacing. Mrs. McDonald was right, the floorboards did squeak. She was probably keeping the entire household awake.

She knew that was exactly what she'd done, when she went for a cup of tea at dawn and found Mrs. McDonald already seated at the dining room table.

''You're leaving,'' she said, her expression surprisingly compassionate.

Marilou didn't even bother to ask how she knew. ''If someone could drive me into Cheyenne, yes.''

''If you're sure it's what you want, I'll have one of the men take you.'' She watched Marilou for several minutes before she finally set her cup on the table and leaned closer. "You're doing exactly what he expected you to do, you know. You're walking out on him."

Startled by the assessment, Marilou stared at her. "He all but told me to go."

"I don't think so. I think he let you see every one of his fears, showed you his vulnerabilities and then waited for you to hurt him, just the way the rest of us have. You're going to do it, too."

As the gently spoken accusation ripped into her, Marilou buried her face in her hands. Was that what she had done? Had she been so dead set on not compromising her own principles that she'd failed to see that Cal was simply testing her? Would her leaving mean she'd failed him?

"I have to risk it," she said miserably. "Unless he honestly recognizes our love, unless he allows himself to trust in it, there will always be tests, and he'll always set them up so that I'll fail. He has to admit first that he really loves me. Then, maybe, we'll have a chance."

"You do really love him, then?"

"More than anything," she said. "Enough to leave him."

Mrs. McDonald shook her head. "How did you get to be so stubborn when you're not even a Whitfield or a McDonald?" she asked with a rueful grin.

"Years of practice and spending a month around Cal. He seems to have that effect on me."

"You'll be good for him. I trust he'll wake up before long and see that."

"I'm trying very hard to count on that, too," Marilou said, blinking back a fresh batch of tears. "I'd better go now."

"God bless you for bringing him to me, my child. I owe you everything for doing that."

"Your thanks is more than enough." She held tightly to the old woman's gnarled hand. "Love him for me."

"Always, my dear. Always."

Chapter Fourteen

Once Marilou had gone, Cal felt as if the sky had turned a sullen gray. With her soft-spoken accusations and tearful, brave farewell kisses, she'd left him with a lot to think about, none of it pleasant.

Except for the kisses, of course. The memory of those last kisses made him ache with a sweet longing he'd never expected to feel for any woman. Her sensuality, with its delightful mix of shyness and daring, left him hot and needy. Her caring and warmth had stirred a tender side in him and made him hunger for the full-blown joy of her uncompromising love. He was gut-deep lonely for the first time in his life. He could have sworn he'd known loneliness before, but it had been nothing like this.

Maybe, he thought as he prowled the house restlessly, maybe it was time to take the same risk on love that he had always gambled on business.

Maybe, if he hadn't already sent for Joshua, he would have gone running after her, but he felt dutybound now to wait for his friend's arrival. Joshua's mood was going to be foul enough when he discovered what Cal had in mind for him. He clung to the excuse with the desperation of a drowning man. It kept him from making an impulsive decision that was probably based more on hormones than some sudden shift in his psyche.

What he needed, he decided, was a good, hard ride. That ought to use up some of this misdirected energy. He saddled up a stallion with a wild, anxious glint in its eye. He figured their moods matched. With very little prodding, the horse took off at a gallop, racing the wind, racing thoughts that pricked Cal's conscience like barbed wire.

Despite the chase of memories, exhilaration eventually began to replace moodiness. By the time he'd reached the creek where they'd picnicked with his grandmother, he was hot, dusty and tired. As his horse drank thirstily from the creek, Cal sat astride him and surveyed the land that his grandmother continued to insist on deeding to him.

The palette of colors was harsher than those of Florida, the land less lush. Yet he felt an affinity for the barren, wide-open scenery. Maybe there was something to genetics beyond looks and heart disease and the like. Maybe he'd inherited his love of the land from generations of Whitfields after all. It would explain why he'd felt so at home the minute he'd set foot on the land at Silver River Stables, why he'd been drawn to try something so totally alien to his previous business choices.

Even recognizing that his Florida Thoroughbred operation had been an instinctive and wise choice didn't mean it would be equally smart to take over here as well. For one thing, his grandmother was a tough old bird. No matter what she'd said about giving him free rein, chances were good that she'd want to have her say about the decisions. As strong-willed as they both were, they'd be butting heads constantly. He caught himself smiling at the prospect. She'd be a worthy opponent, better than many of the men he'd encountered in boardrooms. It could be fascinating.

Still, he could be setting himself up for heartbreak. He'd spent years thinking of no one except himself. He wouldn't be able to do that if he agreed to his grandmother's terms. They'd be tied together by more than balance sheets and beef prices. She wouldn't tolerate halfway measures. She'd want his soul, his total commitment. Why hadn't Marilou been able to see how intolerable that would be to a man who'd depended only on himself for all these years? Even his grandmother recognized what she was asking. That didn't keep her from making the demand, but unlike Marilou, at least she wasn't blind to the implications.

Still no closer to a decision about that or the woman who'd walked out of his life, he heard the pounding of hooves and looked up to see Garrett riding toward him, her hair tangled and her cheeks flushed from the ride.

"Your grandmother's looking for you."

"I figured she would be. It's been all of an hour since I last checked in."

She cast a reproving glance at him. "Your attitude stinks, mister. No wonder Marilou dumped you," she said bluntly.

"Marilou didn't dump me," he felt compelled to say, clinging to some small shred of pride. "She had to get back to work."

"Right."

Her sarcastic dig, which was closer to the mark than he cared to admit, nagged at him. "You've passed along my grandmother's message like a good employee. You can take off now."

She studied him without moving, unfazed by his nasty mood. "You don't like her much, do you?" she said, seemingly baffled.

Cal was taken aback by her assessment. "Actually, I do," he confessed. "We're a lot alike, maybe too much so."

"Then why don't you treat her with the respect she deserves? Not many men or women could have done what she's done all these years." Her eyes sparked, and she leaned forward as she tried to share her own obviously intense feelings about his grandmother's accomplishments. "Talk to some of the other ranchers around these parts and you'll see what I mean. She has an indomitable spirit, but she's lonely. All I've heard her talk about since I first came here two years ago was what it would be like if she could just find you. Now that you're here, it seems to me like you're breaking her heart."

"I don't mean to," he said candidly. "I'm just not sure I can do what she wants. Your position will certainly be strengthened if I relinquish my rights to this place. Isn't that what you want?"

"Maybe what you or I want isn't so important," she said quietly, then started off. Before he could recover from her final barb, she added, "By the way, your greenhorn friend is here."

"Joshua? I wasn't expecting him until tomorrow."

"Apparently your employees jump to do your bidding, just like we do around here at your grandmother's. I think maybe you should have warned him about this place. He seemed to go into shock when one of the cows wandered over to check him out."

Cal laughed. "Joshua could do with a few surprises in his life."

Suddenly she was chuckling with him. "Judging from the horrified expression in his eyes, I'm not sure he'd agree."

"I'm sure he wouldn't."

She seemed to relax in the saddle. "Are you coming back now?"

"I'm inclined to let him get better acquainted with the cows first."

"He may quit on you," she warned.

"He might at that. Then again, if he's gotten a good look at the fringe benefits, I'm sure he'll stick around." With a wink, he spurred his horse and took off across the fields, Garrett in hot and furious pursuit.

"I am not a fringe benefit," she shouted, the complaint merging with his laughter as both were carried away on the wind.

Joshua was, indeed, looking a little grim. Cal found him pacing in the parlor, his expression murderous. Since he had deliberately provoked Garrett into running off, he was left to face his friend alone. Not even his grandmother was around to serve as a buffer.

"Are you out of your mind?" Joshua demanded as he came into the room. He ignored Cal's outstretched hand.

"What's the problem?" Cal inquired innocently.

"Just for starters, there are no nonstop flights between Orlando and this godforsaken hellhole."

"I offered to send my plane for you."

"Right. The one with the pilot who thinks he's still flying Medevac helicopters in Vietnam."

"Who better to get you to a hellhole? Any other complaints?"

"Dozens, and that doesn't include the ones I'm anticipating. Why am I here?"

"My grandmother could use a little help with the books."

"I'm quite sure there are adequate accountants in this part of the world."

"None with your expertise or loyalty."

Joshua wagged a warning finger at him. "Don't count too heavily on the latter."

"Oh, but I do, my friend."

"How has your grandmother gotten along all these years without an accountant?"

"By her wits, I suspect. Certainly not by any understanding of accounting procedures as you and I know them. Will you help, Joshua? I can guarantee it will be a challenge, even for a man with your skills."

Joshua sank down in a chair. "Do you realize there is not a drop of Scotch in this house?"

"Play your cards right and I'll sneak some in for you. Will you help?"

He threw up his hands in a gesture of resignation. "Oh, what the hell. As long as I'm here, I might as well give it a shot. What's your stake in this?"

"She wants to leave the place to me."

Joshua's eyes widened. "Good Lord, as if your Florida place weren't enough of a headache. How do you feel about that?"

"I'm not sure yet. At first I was adamantly opposed to the idea, but Marilou managed to get in a few good zingers about my cowardice before she left..."

"She's gone?"

He nodded glumly. "Back to Atlanta."

"For good?"

"Based on the things she said as she flew out here, I'd say the move is permanent."

"How do you feel about that?"

"It was her choice."

"You sound as if you expected her to make it."

"I saw it coming, yes."

Silence fell as Joshua studied him consideringly. "Are you so sure you didn't back her into a corner until it was the only choice she could make?"

"Meaning?"

"You're not stupid, Cal, even if you do choose to live in the oddest places. I'm sure if you think about it, you can figure it out."

After several more uncomfortable days of self-examination, he eventually realized what Joshua meant. He'd been so terrified of losing Marilou that he'd been the one to force her to break it off. That idiotic speech he'd made about living together without commitment had been guaranteed to drive her away. Her departure had only confirmed his general opinion that women always ran when things got tough.

Now that she was gone, he was already restless and bored with trying to make sense of his grandmother's cattle operation. Even with the haphazard bookkeeping and his lack of expertise in the beef market, it wasn't much of a challenge. He hadn't given a thought to Silver River Stables in days, despite repeated calls from Chaney. He'd been reading the *Wall Street Journal* with an eye toward finding something new.

But Joshua's pointed remark had underscored what he'd been thinking earlier that very day: he would always be quick to run unless he finally took the biggest risk of all and admitted to Marilou that he was in love with her.

She had brought excitement to every minute he'd spent with her. Her innocence and enthusiasm had made every day unique, jammed every hour with special moments. He didn't need another new business. He needed the one woman who could make him look at life in a new way, who could teach him the real meaning of family and love and commitment.

And he'd waited far too long to tell her that.

"I'm leaving tomorrow," he told his grandmother and Joshua at dinner that night.

"Leaving?" Joshua repeated, his expression horrified. "Without me?"

"You'll survive."

"Where are you going?" his grandmother asked, her demeanor instantly stiff.

"Atlanta."

At that her disapproval vanished. "It's about time. For a while there I was worried you weren't going to see what's plain as day."

He shook his head and sighed. "I'm surprised you didn't point it out."

She patted his hand. "Some things a man has to figure out for himself."

Marilou was flat-out miserable. In the month she'd been away from Atlanta the rain had finally quit and the skies were a clear blue, but she felt every bit as depressed as she had before she'd gone away. She couldn't get Cal out of her mind. She'd even planted a damned vegetable garden on the balcony of her apartment. The tomatoes were taking over. At least, she thought they were tomatoes. Maybe it was the zucchini that was going nuts.

She'd taken to scouring the sports pages for stories on racing. She'd even picked up *The Daily Racing Form,* which had aroused all sorts of curious stares at work, since the nearest track was in Alabama. She hadn't found one single word about Silver River Stables or Devil's Magic or any of the other horses. There were rumors that a well-respected trainer was in negotiations with an Ocala Thoroughbred breeder, but the reports were so vague that she couldn't be sure Cal was involved.

Half a dozen times she'd picked up the phone to call Florida or Wyoming. Each time, she'd cradled the receiver without dialing. Each time she'd told herself she had to wait for Cal to make the first move.

Telling him goodbye that night had very nearly killed her and, judging from the pallor of his complexion and the set of his lips as he'd heard her out, it had been no easier on him. Still, he had let her go. As his grandmother had warned her, he'd probably told himself a hundred times since then that he was better off without a woman who found it so easy to cut the ties between them.

With her mind only half on her job, she was sorting through the endless stacks of mail in search of something that would engage her interest, when Helen came over, a bemused expression on her face.

"Where'd you go on your vacation? Weren't you in Wyoming?"

"Part of the time."

"I think this letter's for you, then. What kind of crazy guy would take a chance on getting it to you this way? Must be a real romantic."

Puzzled, Marilou held out her hand. As soon as she saw the pale blue vellum envelope, her heart began to thud. The stationery wasn't all that uncommon, but coupled with Helen's remarks, there was little doubt about who had sent it. The last time she'd seen this paper, postmarked from Cheyenne, her whole life had taken an incredible new turn. She turned it over and over, almost afraid to open it.

On the front of the envelope, written not in the shaky hand of Mrs. McDonald but in Cal's bold strokes, were simply her name and Atlanta, Georgia. It was an address so incomplete that it virtually guaranteed it would wind up here in the dead letter office.

The message inside would have provided few clues about the sender to any clerk other than Marilou: I love you. Marry me. Cal.

She felt her pulse soar. Beaming at Helen, she rushed to her supervisor and pleaded for a break. "I have to make a call. It's important."

"Ten minutes," he growled. "And don't expect another one in an hour."

"I promise."

She practically ran to the pay phone down the hall and punched in Cal's Wyoming number. "Elena, it's Marilou. Could I speak to Cal, please?"

"*No está aqui, señorita.* He go away."

Her spirits plummeted. "Away?"

"*Si.* You wish to speak to *la señora?*"

"No. Just give her my love." The minute she'd hung up, she redialed, this time to the farm in Ocala. "Chaney, it's Marilou."

"Hey, gal, we miss you down here. You still in Wyoming with Cal?"

Her spirits nose-dived. Cal must not be there, either. "No, I'm back in Atlanta. Cal's apparently left Wyoming, too. Isn't he there?"

"Nope, we ain't seen hide nor hair of him since the two of you took off. Don't know how he expects me to run this place when he don't even call in or take the calls I make."

"I'm sure he trusts your decisions, Chaney. Do whatever you think is right. How's Dawn's Magic?"

"Growing like a danged weed. You coming back to see her?"

"Maybe," she said wistfully, clinging more tightly to the letter.

"You want me to give the boss a message if he does finally take it into his head to call?" he asked grumpily.

"No," she said. "No message."

Thoroughly dispirited, she replaced the receiver and turned to go back to work.

"You looking for me by any chance?"

She whirled around at the sound of Cal's voice and found him lounging against the wall, dressed like she'd never seen him before. His suit was boardroom gray, his shirt a pristine white, his tie a vibrant and daring red. The man looked like business, but the gleam in his eyes was something else entirely. Something dangerous. Something wicked.

Something vaguely vulnerable.

"You're here," she said, breathless with amazement and excitement. Her heart skittered crazily, and she jammed her hands in her pockets to keep from grabbing the man right here in the hall.

He straightened up and took a step toward her. "Seemed to me that a man ought to be in the vicinity when he proposes, just in case the woman decides to say yes."

She ran her tongue over lips gone suddenly dry. Cal's eyes were locked on the tantalizing gesture. He swallowed hard and took one more step. Marilou felt the wall against her back and Cal's heat less than a heartbeat away.

"I do like a man who anticipates all the possibilities," she said, breathless.

"Enough to marry me?" he said, and that whisper of vulnerability came back.

"Certainly enough to give it some thought," she said, her expression all tease and challenge.

The expression on Cal's face then told her he was past playing games. "It took me a long time to get to this point, Marilou."

"Some might say too long," she agreed.

"Don't go playing coy with me. My heart can't take it."

"Neither can mine," she admitted, moving away from cool tile and into the warm circle of his embrace.

"Is that a yes?"

Her arms went around his neck. "Yes, yes, yes."

She was lost in Cal's kisses when she heard the shocked voice of her supervisor. "Miss Stockton, is this any way to conduct yourself on government time?"

She promptly and dutifully tried to wriggle free, but Cal's arms held tight. "Miss Stockton is no longer on government time," he said. "From now on she's on mine." Apparently he heard her quick intake of breath, because he met her eyes. "That okay with you, Miss Stockton?"

After barely an instant's hesitation, she threw the last trace of caution to the winds. "That is very much okay with me."

Before her boss could react, Cal had scooped her up in his arms and carried her out of the building. "I know that carrying the bride across the threshold is supposed to come after the wedding, but I'm anticipating. You don't suppose we could get married yet today, do you?"

"Are you afraid if we wait you'll change your mind?"

"I'm more worried that you'll come to your senses."

"Not a chance. I love you, Cal Rivers. I always will."

"Don't promise always," he pleaded. "Just today."

She touched a silencing finger to his lips. "No, my dearest Cal, always." She sealed the promise with yet another bone-melting, breath-stealing kiss. "By the way, in case it's of any interest, that man you just insulted back there was a notary."

Cal looked dismayed. "Think he'd forgive me long enough to perform a wedding ceremony?"

"He might be more inclined to forgive you if you let me finish working today."

"I'm afraid his price is way too high. We'll just have to wait. Besides, I think it might be nice to have a real family wedding in Wyoming. How would you feel about that?"

"I can't imagine any place I'd rather have a wedding. What about you?"

"I think I'd feel as if I'd finally come home."

"Do you mean that?"

"I've learned one thing over the past couple of weeks. Wherever *you* are will always be home to me. Besides, I think my grandmother ordered the cake the day I flew off to get you. She'll be horribly disappointed if we don't show up so she can make a fuss over you."

"How long do you suppose this fuss will take?"

Cal grinned at her. "No more than twenty-four hours, if I have anything to say about it."

"That sounds just about right to me, too," she agreed. "What shall we do in the meantime?"

"I have a few ideas," he said, and whispered several in her ear.

"I do like your ideas."

"I thought you might," he said, as he tucked her into the back of a limousine. He assured her he'd chosen the vehicle specifically for its very dark tinted windows. "I wasn't sure I could wait to get you home."

She smiled slowly and reached for his tie. "Tell the driver just to keep going until he hears from you again."

"That could be days," Cal said.

"Then tell him he might as well aim this thing toward Wyoming."

Epilogue

First Saturday in May, Three Years Later

It was not yet dawn when Cal pulled into the stable area at Churchill Downs. Mist still hovered in the air, creating an eerie ambiance. There was something almost mystical about this time of day at any backstretch in the country, but on the day of the Kentucky Derby an indefinable stir of excitement was added. Even the horses seemed aware of it, their ears pricked, their prancing steps livelier. The stable boys and grooms moved just a little faster to complete their chores. The hot walkers and exercise riders talked odds. The trainers definitely paced more nervously. Only the owners, most of them far more jaded than Cal, were still sound asleep in their fancy Louisville hotel suites, recovering from the previous night's Derby festivities.

Cal hadn't slept a wink. Neither had Marilou. They had passed the night making love, making promises, perhaps even making the baby that would be the start of their family. It was barely four-thirty when Cal rolled out of bed and headed for the shower. Marilou had joined him, but for once they were too excited about the rest of the day to lose track of time in each other's arms yet again.

In denims and boots, they left the car and went to the stall where Dawn's Magic was dining on a special blend of grains in lieu of her normal early-morning workout. The filly whinnied when she saw Marilou, bobbing her head until Marilou held out a hand filled with chunks of carrot, her favorite treat.

"You are spoiling that horse outrageously," Cal said.

"How do you know these carrots don't provide the precise incentive she needs to win these big races? Are you willing to tamper with a successful formula?"

"I know I'm not," Reeve Bennett said, joining them. The trainer had been hired by Chaney and Cal after an illustrious career in California. Dawn's Magic was their first Triple Crown contender, though by no means the first major stakes horse Cal had bred. "Morning, you two. Couldn't you sleep?"

"You have to be kidding," Marilou said. "I didn't want to miss a second of this."

"Which reminds me," Cal said. "I have something in the car for you." He returned in minutes with a large package tied with a big red bow. Dawn's Magic seemed to feel the ribbon was for her. She kept stretching her long neck in an attempt to nab it.

"Oh no you don't," Marilou said with a chuckle. "This is *my* treat. You've already had yours." She tugged the ribbons loose and opened the box. Nestled amid the foam chips and tissue paper was a new camera, a top-of-the-line professional model. Her gaze rose to meet Cal's. Again she caught that wavering uncertainty that came far less frequently now.

"I called all over the place to find out the best model. If it's not what you want, you can trade it in."

"It's wonderful," she reassured him. "Thank you."

"I thought today might be a good day for you to finally begin that career you've put off. I'm having a darkroom built on the back of the house while you're gone. You could do conformation photography. Goodness knows there are plenty of horses around. Or you could do studio work. If you want that, we'll put on another room. Do you really like it?"

Tears sprang to her eyes. If she hadn't been holding such an incredible piece of equipment, she would have dumped it on the ground in favor of throwing her arms around her husband. "You couldn't have given me anything I would like more."

"There's film in it already. You'd better get started if you want to catch all of Dawn's Magic's big day. I don't think Reeve is likely to wait around for you to get ready."

Marilou spent the next two hours getting a feel for the camera. Cal had obviously anticipated her fascination. He'd bought rolls and rolls of extra film. By the time they left to change for the race, she had already shot close to a hundred pictures and couldn't stop talking about every one of them.

When they returned to the suite, though, she put the camera on the dresser and went to Cal, sliding her arms around his neck. She molded her lips over his, teasing his mouth with her tongue until she heard the soft moan low in his throat and felt his whole body shudder.

"Some thank-you," he murmured huskily.

"There's more where that came from," she said, nudging him toward the bed.

"Marilou..."

"Hmm," she said, as she tipped him backward until he was sprawling across the still-rumpled sheets. She reached for his boots.

"Sweetheart..."

"Yes, love?"

"We don't have time..."

"You have to change," she reminded him innocently. "I'm just helping."

Her hand reached just a little high before she slid it slowly down his thigh, then on down to the other boot.

"You are not helping."

"Of course, I am," she said, tugging off the boot. Her fingers slipped inside the cuff of his jeans as she reached for his socks. Her nails raked gently down his calves, before she bared his feet, then kissed each toe.

Cal's protests seemed to have lost steam. The heat in the room had gone up by several degrees. She reached for the buckle on his belt. Cal cleared his throat.

"I think maybe I ought to get that."

"No, dear. You just rest."

"Marilou, I am not resting. Resting is a body's natural quiet state. My nerves are on full alert."

"Really? That's nice."

"You have turned into an incredible tease."

"Are you complaining?"

"Not about the teasing. Your timing could do with a little work. We need to be back at the track in exactly one hour."

"We'll be there."

"But in what condition?"

"If you'll be a little cooperative here, I'll have us out of here in no time."

Cal's body bucked as she very, very slowly pulled down the zipper on his pants. "Holy... Okay, wench, enough," he said, grabbing her wrist and pulling her down on top of him. In less than a heartbeat, she was flat on her back, her hands pinned above her head, Cal, half-dressed, looming over her.

"Let's see if I understand this technique," he said, freeing her hands long enough to run his knuckles along the open throat of her blouse. When the caress slowed at the first button, he followed up with a kiss. One at her throat. Then another fraction of an inch lower. Then another, peppering them across her chest until she was writhing beneath him.

"How am I doing?" he inquired with lazy good humor.

"Like a pro," she said, working on the buttons of his shirt and fanning her hands across his bare chest until she could reach every square inch of burning flesh with hungry kisses.

The game flew out of control with his first, hot claiming of her breast. Suddenly slow became needy, then need turned to urgency. Their remaining clothes were nudged just far enough out of the way to allow Cal to drive into her with a white-hot fervor that sent Marilou quickly into a shattering, earth-moving climax. Still in the throes of passion, she arched her hips up, giving back to Cal all the love, all the commitment he had dared to give her.

Slowly their breath returned to normal, their hearts beat in a gentler rhythm, their skin cooled. But still they didn't move, Cal's weight crushing her into the bed, his legs tangled with hers.

"I'm getting far too old for this," he said at last, levering himself up and trying to figure out where her clothes ended and his own began.

Marilou chuckled. "Lordy, I hope not. I'm not even thirty yet and I have no intention of stopping with just one baby."

"Then you'd better hope you're pregnant now. I figure I've got another year, maybe two before you exhaust me. Maybe you could manage twins. That would save a little on the wear and tear."

"Say that when they both start teething at the same time," she teased. "Get moving, love. We now have exactly twenty-seven minutes to get back to the track. I don't want to miss one single second of Derby Day."

"You should have thought of that before you decided to have your way with me," he grumbled just as the phone rang. Marilou reached for it, but he beat her to it then waved her toward the shower.

They were only ten minutes late to the track. Chaney was waiting for them, looking uncomfortable in a suit. He kept running a finger around the collar of his shirt and tugging on his tie.

"You look very handsome," Marilou told him.

"Don't see why I had to get dressed up like this. Only time I ever wear this suit is for funerals and weddings."

"Well, today you're going to be wearing it in the winner's circle," Marilou declared. "What are the odds on our baby?"

"She's a long shot, just like you knew she would be. Thirty-to-one in the morning line."

"That's okay," Marilou said confidently. "That just means we'll make more money betting her."

"You know, missy, I wouldn't go getting your hopes too high. She's a danged good horse, but it's a tough race for a filly to win."

Marilou kissed his leathery cheek. "Care to go for a little side wager?"

He shook his head. "No way. You have a way of getting what you want out of life."

"I haven't got you fixed up with a good woman yet," she said, deliberately taunting him.

He scowled at her. "And you ain't going to, either. You just stay out of my love life and I'll keep out of yours. Go take your pictures, girl. Maybe it'll keep you out of mischief.''

Cal rejoined her then and linked his fingers through hers. "Ready to go to the box?"

She could feel the restrained excitement that practically vibrated through him. She squeezed his hand. "Let's do it."

As they walked into the clubhouse, they were met by noise. Thousands were jammed into the stands and filled the infield. Mint juleps seemed to be the drink of the day, though Marilou was far too nervous to consider putting alcohol on a stomach that was already rolling. As they cut a path through the crowd to the box Cal had taken, Marilou's gaze suddenly shot ahead and found the tall, staid form of his grandmother. Though the older woman tried hard to maintain a disapproving frown, excitement snapped in her eyes as she drew Cal into an embrace.

"Thank you for coming," he said.

"I figured if this was something you insist on doing, I'd better know why," she said. "You say this horse of yours is good?"

"The best," Marilou told her.

"Then if I put two dollars on her to show, I won't be wasting my money?"

Cal grinned. "That kind of bet won't make you rich, Grandmother, but it should be safe enough. Where's Joshua? I thought he was bringing you."

"He dropped me off. Said he had an errand to run. I expect he'll be back before too long."

Just then they heard his voice. "I'm here," he said, edging his way toward them.

Marilou turned around, a smile on her face. Then she caught Cal's expression. He appeared stunned. His grandmother turned pale, then sank into her seat.

"What is it?" Marilou said, taking an instinctively protective step closer to Cal.

He swallowed hard, his gaze never shifting away from Joshua and the two people behind him. Marilou hadn't even realized they were all together until she'd seen Cal's expression.

The woman wore a floppy white hat, a lovely silk dress and shoes that had probably come from the designer salon at Neiman-Marcus. She exuded money and self-confidence. The man, who stood shoulder to shoulder to her in height, was gray-haired and hesitant, though he had a glint of sharp intelligence in his eyes that age hadn't dimmed.

"Hello, Mother, Father," Cal said, his voice tight as he directed a forbidding look at Joshua.

"Your parents," Marilou breathed. When Cal remained stiffly silent, she introduced herself, then stepped aside so they could enter the box. There was another flaring of tension when they spotted Mrs. McDonald.

Joshua caught Marilou's elbow and pulled her back when she moved to join them. "Cal's probably going to have my hide for this, but I thought it was time."

She grinned at him. "You weren't thinking of running out on us now, were you?"

He grinned back. "Actually, I planned to do exactly that. You'll need the seats. Cal intended them for me and my date. All things considered, I think I'll be safer down at the rail."

Marilou let him go, then went to her seat at Cal's side. She tried to make small talk, but everyone was too tense to respond. It was only when the bugle blew to announce that the horses were coming onto the track for the Derby that they began to relax. Cal's father asked about Dawn's Magic. Marilou told about watching the horse being born. Cal talked about his breeding. Marilou took bets for all of them into the clubhouse windows and placed them. By the time she came back, some sort of uneasy truce seemed to reign.

"She looks good," Marilou exclaimed when Dawn's Magic stepped onto the track as the strains of My Old Kentucky Home wafted through the air. "Don't you think she looks wonderful?"

Cal managed a grin. "The fact that she's here at all is an honor," he reminded her.

"I don't want to hear that garbage. You sound like Chaney. She's going to win the race." She smiled at him impishly. "And I'll beat you down to the winner's circle."

His arm circled her waist. "That's a bet."

While Cal focused his binoculars on the post parade, Marilou attached her telephoto lens and snapped pictures. It seemed to take only seconds before the horses were in the gate.

"They're off!" the track announcer said, and a roar went up from the crowd.

Dawn's Magic broke well from her gate on the out-side and moved quickly to a slot just off the lead. It was exactly where Reeve had wanted her. The track was fast, not muddy, but the filly wasn't used to hav-ing dirt kicked in her face. He'd worried what she would do if she fell back too far. She was in third and only three-quarters of a length off the pace as they rounded the first turn.

"She's going to do it," Marilou said confidently.

"Sweetheart, it's a long race," Cal warned.

"But she's like me. We're both the kind who go the distance."

"If she has your heart, then she'll definitely take it," he said, giving her a quick squeeze before return-ing his attention to the backstretch, where two of the favorites were beginning to make their moves. His grandmother's gaze was riveted on the pack of horses speeding for the next turn. As they came flying around the far side of the oval track, Dawn's Magic was al-most neck and neck with the leader.

"Come on, baby," Marilou whispered, her camera forgotten. "You can do it."

Cal went absolutely still as the horses turned for home. Dawn's Magic's fell back to third, and Mari-lou's heart sank. That usually spelled the beginning of the end. Horses often gave up after falling behind.

"Come on," she pleaded, her hands clenched. Cal took one of them and massaged the tension away, un-til she folded her hand around his. Dawn Magic's jockey showed her his whip then, flicking her lightly on the neck. The gallant horse dug deep into some inner reserve and began to move, a thousand pounds of incredible muscle supported by frail ankles and driven by heart.

With less than a length to go, she had caught up with the favorite and the crowd was going wild. Marilou strained but couldn't hear the final call as they tore across the finish line. Her gaze shot to Cal's, as did everyone else's in the box. The tote board flashed Photo in giant letters to indicate that it was too close to call. The stewards would review films again and again, checking for the fraction of an inch between victory and defeat.

As if he couldn't bear the waiting, Cal focused his binoculars again on the horses as they were riding out around the far side of the track.

"Is she okay?" Marilou asked him, her heart in her throat.

He grinned and shook his head. "Looks to me like she'd like to go for another quarter mile or so."

"I told you," she said. "I told you she had it in her."

He hugged her. "So you did."

Just at that instant, Dawn's Magic's number twelve went into the first place spot on the tote board. The stands exploded with sound—cheers from those with winning tickets and even appreciative applause from those who'd recognized that Dawn's Magic had the makings of a Triple Crown champion.

Cal grabbed Marilou's hand and started from the box. Marilou held her breath and sent him a silent message. After just an instant's hesitation, he turned to his family.

"Come with us," he said, his voice choked. "This should be a family celebration."

Marilou reached for his grandmother's arm and helped her up, but then his mother slipped into place on her other side. "Let me walk with you, Mother," she said hesitantly. "We have a lot to talk about."

A slow smile spread across Mrs. McDonald's face, and she winked at Cal. "Maybe we'll talk about me buying into that Thoroughbred operation of yours," she said slyly.

Cal linked his arm through hers. "The only way you're getting a piece of that action, Grandmother, is at the two-dollar window."

Marilou listened to the start of the familiar bickering, felt the slow easing of twenty years of tension, and kept her eyes on the love that was finally flowering again. It would need a lot of tending, a lot of nurturing, but it would grow. She would do her best to see to it.

Family, she thought with a tug of real longing. Then Cal reached for her hand and the longing fled, chased away forever by the strong, loving man at her side.

For years afterward, that moment would be captured for her with one snap of the track photographer's shutter. Five people, eyes brimming with tears, smiling and holding hands while Dawn's Magic nuzzled Marilou's pocket for the carrot that was hidden there.

* * * * *

*If you want to read more about
Joshua Ames and Tracy Garrett, look for
JOSHUA AND THE COWGIRL, coming this
autumn from Silhouette Special Edition.*

FOUR UNIQUE SERIES
FOR EVERY WOMAN YOU ARE...

Silhouette Romance®

Tender, delightful, provocative—stories that capture the laughter, the tears, the *joy* of falling in love. Pure romance...straight from the heart!

SILHOUETTE *Desire*®

Go wild with Desire! Passionate, emotional, sensuous stories of fiery romance. With heroines you'll like and heroes you'll *love*, Silhouette Desire never fails to deliver.

Silhouette Special Edition®

Stories of love and life, these powerful novels are tales that you can identify with—romances with "something special" added in! Silhouette Special Edition is entertainment for the heart.

SILHOUETTE·INTIMATE·MOMENTS℠

Enter a world where passions run hot and excitement is the rule. Dramatic, larger-than-life and always compelling—Silhouette Intimate Moments will never let you down.

SGENERIC